For Jane

J A C K P O T

a novel by Tsipi Keller

S P U Y T E N   D U Y V I L

New York City

Spuyten Duyvil, PO Box 1852, Cathedral Station, NYC
10025; http://spuytenduyvil.net; 1-800-886-5304

Thank you, DeAnna Heindel

Library of Congress Cataloging-in-Publication Data

Keller, Tsipi.
  Jackpot : a novel / by Tsipi Keller.
    p. cm.
      ISBN 0-9720662-1-7
1. Americans--Caribbean Area--Fiction.
2. Women--Caribbean Area--Fiction.
3. Caribbean Area--Fiction. 4. Prostitution--Fiction.
5. Gambling--Fiction. I. Title.
PS3611.E43 J36 2004
813'.6--dc21   2003009345

Jackpot

W HEN MONEY is a given, when your spirit is unencumbered, and your mind free of relentless and demeaning bookkeeping, how easy it is to have style. How easy to acquire taste when your resources are limitless, when you come from a home where luxury is perceived as absolute necessity, very much like fresh air.

Allowing herself a subdued, contented groan, Maggie stretches out on the armchair, as if to extract the optimum, soothing comfort the soft leather affords. With loving, covetous eyes, she takes in Robin's palatial living room, Robin's tall glass doors which lead to the balcony beyond. The balcony, Maggie knows, overlooks the East River, so velvety dark and menacing at this hour. Her entire apartment could fit in this room, and the armchair alone is worth more than the sparse, second-hand furnishings she has haphazardly put together in her own home. At least, she muses with a touch of self-deprecating irony, she has it in her to appreciate beautiful things.

It is Sunday evening. Tomorrow is Monday. Maggie abhors the fact that a new week is about to begin. She hears the blender going in the kitchen and feels a certain vindication tinged with gratitude for Robin who is laboring on her account, mixing frozen margaritas. Maggie would have been satisfied with a simple glass of wine, but Robin, magnanimously, suggested margaritas, and Maggie, thinking of the cold wind blowing outside, hesitated a moment, still opting for wine, but then said yes, she would have a margarita.

"All set," Robin's voice rings out as she marches into the room, carrying a tray; Maggie, ever so imperceptibly, straightens up in the chair. In her cashmere turtleneck and leather mini-skirt, Robin looks her chic and sexy best, and

Maggie's heart swells with envy and admiration. She now regrets not having bothered to change into something more seductive than her black jeans and sweater before leaving the house. How does she expect to attract attention to herself when she goes out, especially with Robin at her side, if she doesn't put more effort into it?

Robin has set the tray on the low coffee table and now kneels down on the carpet, picking up the blue glass decanter and pouring their drinks into beautiful matching goblets. Robin's every gesture is assuredly poised as if, like a geisha, she's been versed, from a very young age, in the high art of entertaining guests. Kneeling down as she does she epitomizes the accomplished, gracious hostess; Maggie looks forward to the day when she, too, will be established in such, or perhaps even grander, surroundings where, at last, she'd have the opportunity to reveal her exceptional gifts.

"I just *know* you'd love the Bahamas," Robin says, handing Maggie her drink. "Just think. The water is so warm and caressing, and we both know how much you love the water."

Robin's voice is also warm and caressing, and Maggie is pleased by the notion that her likes and dislikes are important enough to earn Robin's attention.

"That I do," Maggie says, letting out a short laugh. "I love the water." She takes a careful sip of the icy margarita, remembering not to swallow too fast. "It's delicious," she says.

"I'm glad." Robin tears open a pack of M&Ms and sprawls herself on the leather couch. "I've never steered you wrong, have I? Paradise Island is a dream, and it's so close! A couple of hours on the plane, and we're there, in Paradise." She smiles at Maggie, and Maggie marvels again at how Robin's eyes are always bright and shiny, as if reflecting some pure, inner light. Which is a source of confusion to Maggie because she knows that Robin is far from pure.

"Did I tell you?" Robin pauses a moment. "Last time I was there"—she pops a couple of M&Ms into her mouth—"I fucked my brains out, *and* gambled a lot. I even made some money which helped pay for my trip."

As if mesmerized, Maggie watches the M&Ms disappear in Robin's mouth. She mulls over, "fucked my brains out," so casually uttered by her friend. She finds herself admiring the audacity, the implied violence, the hard-core sexuality of those few words. Only Robin could say such a thing without sounding cheap. Robin is too white, too *creamy*, to ever sound cheap. Her good breeding shows on her face, on her smooth skin. Especially tonight, as she sits on her black leather couch, wearing her lavender cashmere turtleneck.

Robin can afford cashmere: on top of her salary, she gets a monthly allowance from her parents. Good breeding and class; it is clear that Robin never lacked for anything. Robin, who is secretive about her exact money situation, but lets it be known she comes from wealth, every so often dropping a hint or two about her glamorous parents in L.A. She is lavish when it comes to her own needs, but calculating and quite the tightwad when it comes to others. When Maggie and Robin go out to dinner, Robin orders the most expensive dish on the menu, but never offers to pay more when they split the bill. Often, Maggie resolves that she, too, will order an expensive dish, but can never bring herself to do so, reasoning that by this act of rebellion she'll be only punishing herself, having to pay even more in the end. Resigned, she concludes that some people, people like Robin, are generous to themselves and miserly toward others, while some people, people like her, are generous to others and miserly toward themselves.

Because of her own, not very impressive background,

Maggie feels inferior to Robin, and therefore grateful to have someone like Robin for a friend. They met right after Maggie divorced Tom and moved downtown to start a new life. She and Robin temped for a while at the same ad agency and, thanks to Maggie's persistent initiatives, they kept in touch after their respective assignments ended. With time, they became friends. Close friends, Maggie likes to believe, even if Robin tends to act superior, and sometimes downright condescending. Yet Maggie has trained herself to tolerate Robin's attitude, for the simple reason that Robin is usually right when she criticizes Maggie, and Maggie is eager to learn, she wants to better herself.

As Robin licks her fingers, an image flashes through Maggie's mind and she sees a swollen penis in Robin's luscious mouth. The darkish-reddish intrusion, thrust in Robin's face, disfigures it, and Maggie is filled with revulsion, yet invokes the image again and again, as if compelled. She tries to imagine Robin in bed with a man, and wonders if Robin, or any other woman, actually enjoys having her brains fucked out. Maybe she's old-fashioned, but she still believes in love, true love, and tenderness. Yes, to love someone, someone who would love her back without reserve.

More M&Ms pop into Robin's mouth in quick succession. Robin's teeth, Maggie reflects, must tingle with sugar. Just the thought of it, makes her own teeth hurt. She doesn't want any candy, but wishes that Robin would offer her some all the same.

"So?" Robin says, crunching down on a candy. "Will you come? You love to gamble, Maggie. We'll have fun."

Maggie smiles. How sweet and charming Robin is when she decides to play the part, smiling her beautiful, seductive, somewhat mischievous smile.

"I'd love to go," Maggie says, but is still undecided. In a

couple of weeks, Robin is planning a trip to the Bahamas; she wants Maggie to join her. Presumably to let Maggie share in the fun, but in fact, so Maggie suspects, because Robin does not want to go alone and, travelling with a friend, may get a better package deal. After all, she knows Robin, knows how Robin operates. She has the sense that Robin assumes that her motives remain hidden, which, Maggie thinks, is part of Robin's allure. It's a subtle thing that Robin does; perhaps she doesn't even try to mask her motives.

"Who did you go with last time?"

"With Lucy, I don't think you two have met?"

"No." Maggie has heard of Lucy, but Robin, so far, has kept Lucy to herself; this, Maggie has to admit, she resents a little bit. She is dying to ask why Lucy won't be joining Robin this time around, but is not sure she wants to hear the answer. And yet. "Why don't you ask Lucy to go with you?" she asks.

"Because." Robin smiles, shaking her head and the healthy mass of her wavy, auburn hair. "You're so insecure, Maggie. You think I've asked Lucy, and Lucy refused, right?"

Maggie shrugs, smirking, acknowledging that perhaps Robin has guessed correctly.

"But you're wrong, see?" Robin continues. "I haven't asked Lucy, yet. I'd rather have you come with me."

Maggie is flattered. So, it is all in her head. She must accept the possibility that Robin has no ulterior motives, that Robin is just being Robin, and that her own convoluted thoughts and distrust are a direct result of her middle-class circumstances, circumstances she'd do well to forget and put behind her. She should feel privileged, and frequently she does, that Robin has accepted her as a friend. At times she even wonders why Robin sticks with her.

Maggie muffles a sigh. Such confusion in her head, a sort

of rumble in her chest, and it's all her doing. This is the sort of intricate, maze-like thinking and doubts she has to battle when she is with Robin. "What if we fight?" she asks with sudden clarity; she doesn't want to lose Robin.

"Oh, Maggie, don't be negative."

"You're right." Maggie tries to think. A question still nags at her, and she carefully modulates a light, detached tone. "I guess it's cheaper if you get a friend to travel with you."

Robin jerks her head upward and seems to contemplate the ceiling before lowering her gaze and resting her clear, hazel eyes on Maggie. "Not by much, actually. And money, my dear, is not the issue. I just think it'll be fun for us to spend time together. But don't let me pressure you. You don't have to come if you don't want to, you know."

"I know." Maggie's heart beats a little faster. Invariably, when told she doesn't have to do something, she is tempted all the more. But money, in her case, is the issue. Still, she could manage the trip if she wanted to. And maybe she should, she could use the diversion. Going away with Robin would be fun; Robin would be her guide to new adventures. Her life for the past couple of years has been too sedate: no ups, no downs, just a straight line of work, sleep, paying bills, an occasional dinner out. It's time she woke up. Spending a few days with Robin, she may pick up a couple of essential clues about life, about the future. Robin is a year younger than she, but is mature and worldly and enviably hip. Having landed a job with CBS, she's up on the latest as to the right people, the right look, the right accessories. Maggie, on the other hand, works as a copy editor for a text-book publisher where jeans and sneakers are the norm, and where the people she meets lead the same boring life that she does. Compared to Robin, she really doesn't have a life. And, as far as she knows, she's never fucked her brains out.

Maggie glances at Robin who, like a greedy child, is digging deeper into the bag of M&Ms, an intent expression on her face. Sex is such a mystery, Maggie wants to say, but she knows that Robin won't cooperate. When sex is the topic, Robin radiates a certain attitude, an aura of superiority, which leaves Maggie feeling she's an ignorant fool. She's had what she deems to have been good sex with a couple of partners and, even with Tom, sex was more or less satisfying, at least in the beginning. She has to admit, though, that in her fantasies, sex is much more thrilling, and when she listens to Robin talk about "great" sex, she shrinks inside, feeling inadequate, realizing that perhaps she is missing out, not only on sex, but on life. She's a simpleton, a naif, who has no clue as to what real life, real pleasure, is all about.

One thing is clear: Robin projects a confidence that she lacks. Robin is bold and aggressive in a contemporary way, as featured in the movies coming out of Hollywood, where the women are the aggressors and, in the bed scenes, are always on top. Robin is familiar with the literature, the lingo, the sex toys and, according to her, orgasm is out, control is in. Orgasm, Robin repeats every so often, is not the point.

What do you mean, Maggie will ask, but Robin will only smile, shrug her shoulders, and it occurs to Maggie that Robin, for all her bravura, is stuck in some fetishist stage, that Robin, in fact, cannot come. At such moments she resents Robin for not being truthful, for playing head games with her. And yet, secretly, Maggie wishes she were more like Robin, wishes she could share in Robin's new-world experiences. Robin has had many lovers, while she, well she, compared to Robin, is virtually a virgin. Robin, obviously, has no standards; she'll jump into bed with anyone, to "experience" him. Maggie, just as obviously, is more picky, more cautious. And she likes the guy to be on top, and she wants to come during sex—otherwise, what's the point? As far as control goes, in bed she willingly relinquishes it. At twenty-six, she feels she has yet to taste life, fully. Marriage, she is convinced, has set her back, and the three years with Tom stretch behind her, hanging from her shoulders like a heavy mantle. It was time to shed it, to disengage.

"What if," she asks. "What if we don't meet them? The right guys?"

"What's 'right' Maggie? Leave it to me, we'll meet them." Robin smiles, crushing the plastic bag now empty of M&Ms. "You know what's wrong with you, Mag?"

"No." Maggie smiles back, anticipating a friendly rebuke. "What's wrong with me?"

"You worry too much."

"It's not that, I swear, I was just thinking out loud. Frankly, I don't care one way or the other. If we do or don't fuck our brains out." There, she said it. "I'd be happy just to get away."

"You're lying, my dear." Robin laughs merrily. "Besides, that's not the right attitude."

"But what about AIDS? Don't tell me you don't worry about AIDS."

"Of course I do, but you need to be cautious, use your head. Make sure your guy uses his latex."

My guy—Maggie smiles at the idea. Instantly, the guy appears in her mind. She sees the two of them. The four of them. They stand by the pool, squinting, smiling in the bright sun. She and her guy, Robin and hers. She sees the guys' bare chests, their small, hard nipples, their muscular abs. She even sees the white patches of light, quivering across the turquoise surface of the pool where the sun hits the water. Robin, somehow, always manages to rouse in her the most vivid images.

For this Maggie feels grateful, feels a tenderness toward her friend, which borders on the physical. Yes, she decides, she'll go to the Bahamas. If nothing else, she and Robin will get closer, perhaps share a couple of unique experiences.

She's made up her mind. "I'll go," she tells Robin.

"I knew you would." Robin reaches for a fresh packet of M&Ms. "We'll have fun, I promise."

"I'm sure," Maggie says. "Can I have some?" She points at the M&Ms.

"Of course. Here."

Maggie rises from the chair and walks toward Robin's extended hand. "Just one," she says. "I only want one."

"Oh Maggie, you're a scream." Robin sighs and stretches out on the couch. She gives Maggie a faint smile and shuts her eyes. "God, I'm pooped. You know, Mag, I'm not very hungry anymore. Would you be terribly upset if we don't go out? I wish I could make something for you, but my fridge is boringly empty."

All at once, Maggie feels hollow, irrelevant, standing there, watching Robin disintegrate on the couch, her large breasts, under the fine cashmere, spilling to the sides. What is she to do now? she wonders. Is she welcome to stay or is she invited to leave?

"What do you want to do?" she asks helplessly.

"Nothing, to tell you the truth." Briefly, Robin opens her eyes, then shuts them again. Maggie walks back to her chair and picks up her bag. "I hope you don't mind," she hears Robin say, but doesn't turn around. She does mind, she is hungry, they were supposed to go out, but what's the point of saying so? Eating in, she reminds herself, she'll save a couple of bucks. If she is to go on the trip, better start saving now. And since she's already on her feet, and Robin doesn't insist that she stay, she might as well go home.

"It's all right," she says, trying to put some life into her voice. "I'll have something at home."

"Let me see you to the door." Robin, with exaggerated effort, raises herself from the couch. "I don't know what's the matter with me, but I couldn't go out if you paid me. You sure you don't mind? I feel a little guilty."

"No need to feel guilty. I'm fine, really," Maggie says, but, to her great surprise, as she walks home, tears are rolling down her cheeks. She hates herself for crying, for feeling so small. How silly of her, how immature. It's Robin's fault. No, it's hers. What's wrong with her? She wipes her cheeks and nose with the back of her hand, then wipes her hand on her coat. Just like a baby, she tells herself. Like a teenager. She is not even sad, so why these stupid tears? She feels so aimless inside, so undecided.

Is she crying from relief? Shame? Both? When she stood up to take the M&M from Robin's hand she felt a twitch in her lower back and realized she must have been tense in that exquisite armchair. The truth is: she is always tense around Robin, but tears? That's a bit extreme, to say the least! She'd better get a hold of herself.

I'm going through a phase, she thinks, hoping to quell her agitation and restore some order in her feelings. Lately, she's been filled with tears just waiting to come out. She cried last night when she watched the news on TV and a father held his daughter who had just got the news that her husband had survived some awful accident. Maggie saw a river of love and tenderness in the father's body as he gathered his collapsing daughter into his arms. Such father/daughter scenes always stir powerful emotions in her and her eyes fill up.

But, the good thing is, she is walking, taking one step, then another. It is brutally cold, and she fastens her coat around her. Here, she has calmed down. Just a quick silly attack of overwrought nerves. Once she gets home, between her four walls, she'll feel a lot better. Maybe that's her problem: she finds comfort in being alone.

MAGGIE HEATS UP SOME LEFTOVER meat balls she finds in the freezer, and makes a small salad. She thinks of tomorrow and remembers that what awaits her in the morning is another hateful day at the office, another week of managed abuse at the hands of her boss, Mr. Faber.

She takes her food to the couch and, clicker in hand, goes through the channels. Guns, police cars, commercials. Lots of cable channels to choose from but nothing to watch. Pat Robertson talks into a mike, something about Jesus. She goes through the channels one more time—by now, she hopes, the commercials should be over, perhaps she'll catch a good program. The food she is eating at the low table is warm and satisfying, reassuring. She knows how to draw pleasure from the smallest, simplest things. After dinner, she will go to bed and read for a while.

No, she thinks. She doesn't want to go to bed, yet. She wants to prolong the weekend, her sense of freedom. She remembers a puzzling line from a dream she woke up from yesterday. In the dream, she tells someone, "Tie me up and mail me first-class."

She smiles with affection for herself. It's a funny line and she is glad she has dreamt it. But what could it mean? First

class, obviously, is the key. She wants everything—her life—
to be first class. Right now, it's probably third or fourth class:
slow, gray, and bulky.

There's absolutely nothing on TV. Here's Pat Robertson
again—she is disgusted by the bland, pasty face, the small
eyes, is afraid that her soul will be contaminated if she looks
at him for too long.

"If you engage in murder, and abortion is murder, now is
your time—let Jesus come into your heart. Bow your head
and pray with me. That's right, don't be afraid." Pat shuts his
eyes and calls on the Lord to come into his heart. "Now, go
to the phone and say, I prayed with Pat Robertson, that man
on TV, and I now know the Lord. Go to the phone and make
a pledge."

She switches channels. At this very moment, she reflects,
many viewers actually go to the phone and like automatons
repeat the words: I've prayed, I know the Lord, here's my
pledge. It is hard for her to fathom how they let themselves
be lured into Pat's trap. Pledge is Robertson's true message;
abortion and the Lord, just handy accessories.

She takes the plate to the kitchen and puts it in the sink
on top of the lunch and breakfast dishes—a real mess, a pre-
cariously sloping pyramid. She marvels, yet again, that it
takes so many dishes to feed just one person. She'd better do
them now, or she'll be faced with a sink full of smelly dishes
when she wakes up—a depressing sight on any given morning, but especially on Mondays. Indeed, she should do them
now, but she feels a little lazy, perhaps tired. Lucky Robin has
a dishwasher, a state-of-the-art kitchen, yet Robin never eats
at home. When Maggie was married, she lived with her husband in a one-bedroom apartment on the Upper West Side,
and they, too, had a dishwasher. When they divorced, Tom
was willing to let her have the apartment, but she couldn't

afford it on her own. So the both of them moved out, he to Chicago, she downtown, to a dishwasher-less apartment. Whom could she sue for declining living standards?

She comes out of the kitchen and again goes through the channels. Nothing. She turns off the TV. Bed and book, then. Normally, in bed, she doesn't last very long: as soon as she's horizontal, her eyelids, like a doll's, close. To trick herself, she'll lie on her stomach, and so manage to read a few pages before she absolutely must turn off the light and let herself fall asleep.

She takes off her clothes and crawls into the bed. Brrr, it's cold, but soon she'll be warm, turning herself into a small ball under the cover. Now she questions the wisdom of her going to the Bahamas. She has hardly any money in her savings account, and whatever she has managed to save will be consumed by the trip. But she can't go on living like this, constantly worrying about money. She's made the right decision. She'll go with Robin, she'll get to live a little.

"I'M TAKING A SHORT VACATION, MR. FABER," she tells her boss, who insists that 'mister' be attached, at all times, to his name.

Mr. Faber looks up from his desk, clearly annoyed; she is disrupting his work. Behind his thick glasses, he briefly shuts his eyes and takes a deep breath, pretending to suppress an aggrieved sigh. He is only thirty-five, Maggie reflects, and already an old bore. With his black, wet-looking hair fastidiously combed to one side, his meticulous desk, he's a miserable human being—what on earth could give him pleasure?

"How short?" he asks.

"A week."

"A week." Mr. Faber opens a drawer then shuts it, not saying a word, just letting her stand there and sweat it out.

Why do you have to make me feel shitty? Maggie wants to shout, but then Mr. Faber reaches for his calendar and studies it.

This is his *spiel*, she reflects, his power play. Let him play it, then. She focuses her gaze on the shiny, bald spot at the top of his head. The hopeless pathetic prick. Probably hates his job as much as she hates hers, but he would never admit it, would probably rot in this chair forever, while she, she has other plans, she will look for another job, will become a real important editor, a literary editor. How hard she tried to please him when she first got there, a little over a year ago. How hard she tried to create a friendly rapport, to make her days in the office a little more bearable.

I've already made the reservations, she is dying to tell him, just to annoy him further.

Still studying the calendar, he says without looking up, "I don't know what's the matter with you women, needing to take vacations all the time."

Stunned by the incongruity of the remark, she cannot be sure he actually said it, that she actually heard it. She says nothing, and stubbornly continues to stare at the bald spot. Mr. Faber, like a dutiful boy at school, now stoops over the desk and with his special pen marks the calendar. He writes: "Maggie vacation" then draws an arrow across the dates. She watches the crooked letters form laboriously under his hand, and when the ritual is finally over, she mutters, "Thank you," to the bald spot and leaves his office.

Her desk is a mess. Maybe that explains Mr. Faber's dislike for her. But Susan, the assistant editor, is organized, and he's just as rude, if not more so, to her. Susan is in her thirties, and Mr. Faber, it seems, gets a greater kick from exercising his authority over a more mature person. The man has a problem, and it's not hers; she won't let herself brood about him. Indeed, soon, when she gets around to it, she'll look for another job. Editorial positions are hard to come by, so maybe she'll look for something more glamorous, maybe an ad agency, or a PR firm, where they would train her, where she could build a career for herself, a future. It's time she believed in herself, in her abilities. She'll learn to be aggressive, like Robin, Robin who is out there every day of the week, playing the game among the real power-brokers.

She goes to the bathroom, her place of refuge, where she can be alone for a moment or two. She comes in here quite often, maybe every hour on the hour. Thankfully, there are no unpleasant odors, and there's a full-length mirror where she can look at herself. She wonders how many office workers around the world disappear in bathrooms for a much-needed respite. Probably millions, probably mostly females. If economists applied themselves, they'd come up with a system of checks and balances to figure out the yearly cost of this loss of productivity at the workplace. But the system is so shrewd, maybe this loss is already computed in employees' paychecks, the female employees.

Maggie bends forward at the waist, lets her arms dangle, her hands almost touching the floor. She is limber, and is proud of it. She shuts her eyes—blood throbs in her temples. It's only ten o'clock in the morning; a whole day—a wasteland—stretches ahead of her, to fill in the hours till five o'clock.

AT HER DESK, MAGGIE SCRIBBLES IN A PAD:

> Maybe I am
> too too too
> too much
> alone
> too maybe
> too
> maybe
> too much
> much
> too maybe
> maybe too
> too too too
> much

"WHO'S THERE?" Heart pounding, Maggie sits up in bed. Did she dream it, or did she actually scream? Something has startled her out of sleep, and alarms are sounding off in her head. She looks around her, listening to her heart. It's all right, calm down, she tells herself. False alarm. She is alone.

She sits hunched over, massages her left heel under the cover. Something, someone, grabbed her foot. She felt it so distinctly, the firm grip of a malevolent hand. Staring at the faint gray light in the window, her eyes glaze over. At this early, crystal hour, the sky takes on the cool sharpness of steel. Was it a dream?

It's a good thing she lives in a studio-apartment. From her bed she can survey everything, even see into the bathroom, if the door is open, as it is now. Her tiny kitchen is part of the living area. She could never live in a mansion where too many rooms and stairwells would stand between her and the front door.

From the haze in her mind, another dream surfaces: she and Robin sit and talk in Robin's living room. She needs to go to the bathroom, but holds it in, afraid that the odor of her urine will spread from the bathroom throughout the apartment and reach Robin's nose. Her dreams are so real, so *logical*, no wonder she often questions reality.

She lies back down, pulls the cover toward her. Fear, she reflects. How it rules her life. Has ruled her life from an early age, since that short, dark man grabbed her breasts on her way to school. That a pervert should be out, preying, so early in the morning. A woman, a girl, is always on guard, always looks over her shoulder. It's instinctual, and yet, rational. She was about thirteen or fourteen when it happened, and it changed her, introducing a new kind of fear into her life, a new sense of guilt and awareness. She had just begun to wear a bra, a padded one, and after the initial shock, and the new understanding that she was now a target, she remembers watching with horror as the man's face registered his disappointment when he realized he was clutching a padded bra and not the firm breasts of a young girl. How mortified she was—both by the assault on her person and for being found out. Absurdly, she felt guilty for failing to please him; felt anger and shame and disgust, which she directed at herself for siding with the man against her body. Ever since that morning, when she's out on the street, she's always alert, is always aware of who's behind her. Daytime or nighttime, it makes no difference.

She dozes off for a while, her lids heavy with desire for sleep. She has an image of herself as an old woman, sleeping in her bed. Like her mother, still young but old, dying of cancer. Toward the end, how surprisingly tiny her mother's palm was, so soft and boneless, nearly lifeless. After her mother's death, she told someone she felt as though she were living the P.S. to her life. Of course, it was absurd, she was much too young to feel this way. She tries to remember if she actually said it and to whom. Maybe to Tom? It is amazing to her now that at one point she thought he was the best thing that ever happened to her. At the very beginning, she and Tom probably loved one another; at the very least, that's what she wants to believe. As a matter of fact, she remembers quite acutely loving him. But Tom always claimed she didn't know how to love him, and it baffled her. So she claimed he didn't know how to love her, and they complained and bickered back and forth, a cycle, she is convinced, he had initiated. True love, she always believed, should come naturally, without "knowing," without a formula; obviously, they were not right for one another. He wasn't the worst thing that could have happened to her, but definitely not the best. What is the best thing that ever happened to her? She can't think of any one particular thing. It hasn't happened to her yet, it lies in the future.

S HE IS COUNTING THE DAYS: ELEVEN. One day soon, if not soon enough, she'll wake up in the morning looking forward to the day. Seven a.m. she'll board a plane and fly to Paradise Island. What a fitting name. Just as easily, Robin could have picked Aruba, or some other island, but no, it was meant to be Paradise Island. Maybe it is, was, the original paradise where Adam and Eve and all the animals lived peacefully, and a benevolent God, lazy and out of work, hovered above, cushioned in downy clouds.

"Did you know," she tells Susan, "that Eve was the first explorer?"

"Eve?" Susan says, but remains focused on her computer screen.

"Yes. From the Garden of Eden. She was the first to explore what was around her. Adam was the docile one, content with domesticity."

Susan looks up. "Yeah, so?"

"Nothing. It's just that he was cowardly, too, immediately pointing the finger at Eve when God came looking for them."

Susan laughs, a high, ringing laugh, and Maggie joins in, giggling, glancing in the direction of Mr. Faber's door. And, soon enough, his voice is heard, calling out from his office,

"Susan, come in here, will you?"

The "will you?" is especially grating; Maggie and Susan smirk, roll their eyes.

"Be right there, Mr. Faber." Susan gets up, and Maggie watches her walk into Faber's office. What would happen, she wonders, if Susan were to call back, "I can't talk to you right now, I'm busy."

What if they had an affair? Susan and pathetic Mr. Faber? Susan is looking for a lover. Every week, she consults the personal ads in *New York Press*. In her heart Maggie wishes that Susan will find the man of her dreams. She wishes the same for herself. Maybe she should take her fate in her hands and place an ad in *The New York Review of Books*. She'll simply write: Woman seeks man. You can't get any more direct than that. None of the cute witticism, the feigned lightheartedness of the usual ad. Indeed, when she skims pages of personal ads, she is filled with apprehension, a certain unease. Perhaps because the ads, blocked in dark lines and measured in inches, remind her of obituaries; the rectangles and squares turn into tangible chunks of human- ity. She senses the anguish, the hope, vested in the phrasing, in the placing of each ad. So much depends on them. These small biographies become alive for her, as she envisions the authors and asks herself how honest they allow themselves to be, how honest can they be.

Her prospective ad is as honest as they get: Woman seeks man. When her ad appears, she'll give special attention to the ads that surround hers on the page. If they happen to be by men, she'll write to each of them and say: Hey, our ads were placed side by side, we made contact on the page. So far, she hasn't had the nerve to place an ad or respond to one. For one thing, the city is full of weirdos. For another, from what she hears, the success rate isn't great. Susan has gone out on a few dates, and they were all disasters, as far as love and romance go. But, Susan says, they were worth the try: you get to know what's out there. And even when it doesn't work out, you can always become friends, and so meet new people. When she comes back from vacation, tan and rested and emboldened, she'll respond to a couple of ads, send her picture. Or maybe she won't have to. Maybe she'll get lucky and meet someone in Paradise.

Maggie smiles at her thoughts. Just then, Susan comes out of Mr. Faber's office, writes something on a piece of paper and hands it to Maggie. Maggie reads: "The prick says we talk too much." Maggie writes: "Tell him that's the problem with women, they talk too much, they should have stayed near the stove in their neat aprons." She hands the note back to Susan. Susan reads it, smiles, then tears it up into very small pieces.

"WE'RE BOOKED," ROBIN TELLS HER OVER the telephone. "You can't change your mind."

"I'm not going to." Maggie laughs gaily.

"What's funny?"

"Nothing. I'm just happy. I can't believe I'll be leaving this place. It's my first real vacation in years."

"Good, that's the spirit! Now comes the painful part. You have to mail me a check for seven-ninety-five."

"You? Why not the agent?"

"Because," Robin says. "I charged the whole thing to my

Visa."

Maggie would have liked to charge her part, too, but doesn't want to make a fuss. "All right," she says. "I'll mail it tonight."

"Great," Robin says, and Maggie senses that Robin prepares to get off the phone.

But Maggie wants to talk more, she doesn't want to hang up. "Are you all right?" she asks. "You sound a little....?"

"A little what?"

"Oh, I don't know." Maggie feels awkward for having tried to draw out the conversation, but if they hang up now she'd feel even worse. "Busy?"

"Not more so than usual," Robin says, sounding distant.

"You know, my boss, he wasn't very happy about my taking time off. He said he couldn't understand what was wrong with women, needing vacations as they do."

"What did you say?"

"Nothing. What could I say?"

"Well," Robin says.

"Am I going to see you before we leave?"

"I don't know, sweetie, we'll see."

"I think we should meet, so we can discuss things."

"What things, Maggie? Everything is pretty clear."

"I know. But I think we should discuss the trip."

"There's nothing to discuss. Just pack light. We're not going to check any luggage, just carry-on."

"Of course," Maggie says, and Robin laughs.

"You're such a treasure," Robin says and hangs up.

Eight more days, Maggie thinks. She can't wait. For take-off, for sunshine, for freedom. No Mr. Faber, no subways, no office. It occurs to her that while in Paradise, she'll be doing the same, she'll be counting the days, the hours, but with trepidation, willing them to last. One way or the other, she is always counting, and all because of her employee-life. If only she could find a way to change that one, all-important fact.

"I 'M NOT HAPPY," Susan says softly, matter-of-factly. Mr. Faber is out, and they're sitting at their desks, eating pizza. "I'm not unhappy, I'm just not happy. There's an underlying sadness to everything I do."

"Do you know why?" Maggie asks, cautiously. What Susan says hits too close to home. It frightens her to think that she will end up like Susan, quite attractive but already middle-aged, working in a crummy office, for a crummy boss. Maggie shoos away the thought, somehow convinced it won't happen to her. She has a lot going for her, she is still young. By the time she reaches thirty, or thirty-two, she is sure to make something out of her life.

"I don't know," Susan says. "It's a weird feeling. I do everything I'm supposed to do. I get up in the morning, I come to work, I meet friends for dinner, but the joy is not there. And each day that goes by, I'm keenly aware that another day of my life is over. I used to love my life, but not anymore. Maybe I'm changing."

"Changing, how?" Maggie concentrates on Susan's wrist, so white and delicate and yet strong, as Susan picks up the pizza and brings it to her mouth.

Susan, chewing, shakes her head. "I wish I knew. Maybe that's what they mean by getting old?"

"You're not old." Maggie squirms in her seat. "Maybe you're just tired of living alone?"

"I don't think so." Susan turns pensive. She seems surprised by the suggestion, and Maggie worries that perhaps she's said the wrong thing. "I like living alone."

"Maybe it's a phase, then," Maggie tries to sound cheerful. "It will pass."

"I hope so." Susan sighs. "What about you?"

Maggie shrugs. "What choice do I have?"

"What do you mean?"

"I don't know. I guess I like living alone."

"No, I meant, do you enjoy your life?"

"Yes, I think I do," Maggie says uncertainly. Well, does she, or doesn't she? "Outside the office I do. At least I think I do. I don't think about it much. I mean, I do, I'm sort of thinking that something good is about to happen, if not today, then tomorrow."

"You're still young," Susan says wistfully, and Maggie nods. Maybe she is not so young.

"What are you doing tonight?" Susan asks her toward the end of the day as they prepare to leave.

"Tonight? Nothing."

"Want to go for a drink?"

Maggie thinks. Why not go for a drink? She may meet someone. She is leaving for the Bahamas, she will tell him, sounding worldly, sophisticated. Anybody who is somebody takes a winter vacation. "My winter vacation," she'll say, "but I'll be back." While she's away, he'll be longing for her, and maybe she'll be longing for him, fantasizing about the moment when they re-unite.

"Good idea," she says. "Let's celebrate my trip."

"WHEN ARE YOU LEAVING?" SUSAN ASKS IN THE bar. It is loud, noisy, and they have to shout into each other's ear.

"In a week." Maggie laughs. The noise around them amuses her. There's no loud music or anything, but the level of noise is constant, the sound of many voices climbing over each other, wanting to be heard at once. This is what she likes about city life. The exuberance of office workers, once they're let out. Young men in suits stand all around, a drink in hand. Watching them, she feels ambivalent, an ambivalence she can trace back to her childhood. It's as if she is regarding the enemy, or something she needs to subdue, conquer. And yet, she also envies them, their sure, easy manner, their peace with the physical. Their eyes shine, they seem eager, and when she conjures up their potential chivalry, it stabs at her heart. They're young men at the beginning of their careers. Soon, they'll start a family and be on their way. It is possible that even Mr. Faber is in a bar somewhere, just like this one, showing a different face to those around him. It is possible, but somehow she doubts it.

Maggie feels excitement mount in her. She is young, strong, she loves life. She can do anything she wants. She orders another Screwdriver; Susan is still nursing her first.

"Come on, Susan, drink up."

"Don't worry, I'll catch up."

Again, she looks at the men. They're so busy talking to each other—why don't they talk to her and Susan? Two guys stand so close to them, they could hear what she and Susan are saying, if only they listened.

"Don't you just love it"—Maggie pumps animation into her voice—"the way we come out after work and break loose? It's so easy to forget what you want to forget when you're sitting in a bar and people around you are joking and laughing. As soon as I leave the office, I feel like I'm bursting with energy, like I'm alive again."

"That's great," Susan says, but Maggie can tell Susan's mind is elsewhere. Her enthusiasm is curbed, and she reaches for a cigarette from her pack, sneaking a glance at the two guys. Nothing doing. Now they move away. Robin would have engaged them in conversation, openly challenging them, the way guys like to be challenged. Robin speaks their language, whereas Susan is as inept as Maggie.

Maggie lights the cigarette. "Maybe you too should take a vacation," she tells Susan and, as she says it, she remembers Mr. Faber's comment about women and their incessant need for vacations.

"It's too noisy in here," Susan says. "Let's go to my place. I've cooked a delicious stew, and you've never been to my apartment."

True, Maggie thinks. In fact, it used to bother her that Susan never invited her. But then she realized that she'd never invited Susan either.

"I'll finish my drink." Maggie looks around her. The truth is, she'd rather stay. It's so lively here, potentially exciting.

"Are you sure you want to leave?" she asks Susan.

"I have a headache."

A headache. Women and headaches. Mr. Faber is sure to have something to say about that.

A T SUSAN'S, THEY HAVE BEEF STEW AND salad and polish off a bottle of Merlot, with Maggie doing most of the drinking. Usually, it is a strain for her to feel totally at ease in someone else's home. She always fears she is in the way, perhaps unwanted, perhaps undeserving. But here, with Susan, she feels comfortable, for Susan, so reasonable and calm, seems so straightforward, so uncomplicated. And Maggie likes the apartment—a two-bedroom on West Forty-fifth Street. The rooms are small, and the kitchen is nothing more than a couple of cabinets and a small fridge and stove, and yet, wherever the eye looks it is pleased, for everything looks neat and cozy, with colorful throw-rugs and floor cushions everywhere. One can sense, Maggie reflects, that Susan had a man in mind when decorating her apartment. A man and a home, a cozy retreat. Maggie's apartment, by contrast, still looks as if she has just moved in. A couch, a lamp, a couple of bookshelves—very standard, cold, impersonal, like a motel room. She tells herself and others she doesn't really care about such details, but the truth is she is not quite sure whether she does or doesn't. Maybe she is just being lazy. Maybe she is waiting to move into a better apartment, and then she'll decorate. Somehow, at the moment, she can't be bothered.

"I meant to tell you," Maggie says. "You should have seen our dear Mr. Faber, how he took his time approving my vacation. He looked in his calendar and said, 'I don't know what's wrong with you women, needing to take vacations all the time.' Can you believe it?"

"I believe it." Susan laughs.

"Why do we have to put up with him? Where is it written that if he calls we must drop everything and run to him?"

"It's written across your paycheck, dear. In invisible ink.

Besides, I've seen worse. One day he'll leave for bigger and better things and I'll have his job."

"How do you know?"

"I don't. I'm hoping."

"I don't know if I can wait that long." Maggie picks up her glass of wine. Is she drinking too much, she wonders. She doesn't even like the taste. It's probably a cheap wine for it leaves acrid dregs on her tongue. She begins to hiccup.

"You shouldn't drink so much," Susan says, handing her a glass of iced water.

"I normally don't," Maggie says between hiccups. "I only drink when I go out."

"Still." Susan regards her. "You're quite the drinker for a twenty-five-year old."

"Twenty-six," Maggie corrects, and bites her lip; she wonders if Susan thinks she's an alcoholic. "I learned to drink with my ex," she confides. "He drank every night, so I drank, too." Maggie struggles to keep her breathing even; so many things bubble up to the surface. "He drank much more than I ever did, but then accused *me* of being the alcoholic. I only drink when I'm out with people, when I feel nervous."

"Do you feel nervous tonight?" Susan asks gently.

"A little. Maybe. I always do around people. Like, like I feel I have to talk, make conversation. Or, I don't know, I drink for fun, to generate excitement. I don't know why my ex drank so much. After he went to bed, the TV screen and I became intimate friends."

"Really?" Susan says. "What about sex?"

"Sex?" Maggie snickers. "In the last couple of years, about once every three months, maybe even six."

"You're kidding."

"One night," Maggie continues, almost boasting, "I made love to an orange."

Susan gives her a look. "What do you mean, made love to an orange?"

"I kissed it, with feelings, pretending it was a live thing, a lover. That's another thing about marriage. Your husband goes to bed at eight o'clock, so what do you do? You fantasize about sneaking out and doing something wild, but you stay on the couch. I sat on the couch and snacked some more and watched TV. Of course, I gained weight. Must be a law of nature, marriage and gaining weight—here is a correlation sociologists should sink their teeth into." Maggie pauses; it occurs to her she's never discussed this before with anyone. When asked, she usually lies about her marriage, says it was good, and then they grew apart and went their separate ways, amicably. Which is true: they did part amicably, perhaps indifferently. Or so they both pretended. "Anyway, I was about to peel that orange and eat it? Then it became this thing in my hand and I was kissing it."

Susan laughs, then puts a hand to her mouth. "Sorry," she says, "I shouldn't laugh. It's not funny."

Maggie shrugs. "He said my odor was the problem."

"What odor?"

"My body odor."

"The creep. He actually said that?"

"He did, and you know what, I believed him. I trusted him, you see? I began to rub my skin with all kinds of body lotions, and he watched me go through the whole shenanigans, knowing all along it was a big lie. It wasn't my odor, he just didn't like intercourse. Some kind of vagina-phobia." Maggie twists her lips. She feels a little guilty, exposing him like this; still, he deserves it. "Sometimes, I'd be in the kitchen or living room, and he'd call me into the bedroom where I'd find him on the bed, already erect, ready for me to finish the job. With my mouth. He wasn't vulgar or anything, but when it came to sex, he was sort of infantile. He'd do his share, he'd go down on me, and I grew to like it, actually." Maggie lets out a nervous giggle, feeling herself blush. "A friend had told him that if he went down on a woman, she'd be his forever. Ha! I was married at twenty and divorced at twenty-three. Sometimes, when I think of him, I feel nothing, which makes me think I've lived in a vacuum."

Susan nods. "And your parents?"

Her parents. Maggie picks up her glass of wine. "My mother died when I was seventeen, and my father never said much, he's not the expressive type. He's now remarried and living in Seattle. Men always find someone to marry them. Like my friend Robin says, they look for a nurse and usually find one. She says that a married woman is a stupid woman. We compromise too much, and for what? She says the best strategy is to treat men the way they treat women."

"I don't think I like this Robin, she's bad news." Susan sounds miffed, and Maggie looks up, a little frightened; the last thing she wants is to hurt or upset Susan.

"She is fun," she offers earnestly, "and she is gutsy." And she comes from money, she considers adding, but doesn't. Susan still seems doubtful, so Maggie goes on. "She's a little frivolous sometimes, but she means well. She is smart, and she gets what she wants."

"Are you still in touch? You and your ex?"

"I'm on his Christmas list. His new wife adds a few words to the Hallmark card and he signs it. Like my father, he always gets someone to marry him. He left me all his old records, and I used to listen to them almost every night. Not because I missed him, I just liked the music and the period it reminded me of. I'm still using the pennies he collected in a jar. It's humiliating to think that truth stared me in the face, and I didn't see it."

"You loved him," Susan says. "You wanted to save your marriage."

Maggie shrugs. She doesn't remember thinking in terms of wanting to save a marriage. She remembers Tom insisting she wear a veil or a scarf over her face during sex. He asked her to pretend she was a prostitute or a stranger, seducing him. It aroused him more, he said. It is curious that she is remembering this now. She thought she was done and over with that period in her life. "I don't know what I wanted. I still don't. I don't have a clear idea of the future. It's such a big word, you know, the future?"

"You want love," Susan says.

"Love? No, I don't, I don't think so. Or maybe I do. I want to experience things, meet interesting people."

"Well," Susan says. "I know what I want, but then, I'm a little older than you." Susan smiles wearily. "I want love. I want to get married, I want children."

Maggie nods. She wonders if Susan has always wanted these things, or if they're age-related. "I hope you find the right man very soon."

Susan laughs, and for a moment seems happy as if she's already found him. "I hope so, too. Who are you travelling with, by the way?"

"Robin," Maggie admits hesitantly.

"Are you sure that the two of you would make good travelling companions? Are you good friends?"

Maggie ponders the question. "We're friends. I've known her for a couple of years. We're very different, but on the whole she's all right, she has her moments. Actually, in certain ways, I wish very much I were like her. She's so on top of everything. She's got this fabulous job, this fabulous apartment, the right clothes. She knows how to manage, how to maneuver people. She is sort of ruthless when it comes to getting what she wants. She's like a man, she has guts. She has no scruples." Maggie pauses, debating whether or not she should tell Susan about Robin fucking her brains out. "It's strange, she is younger than me, but when I'm with her, I feel stupid, sort of naive, like a child. And she's great at small talk, she can talk about anything, even with strangers, whereas I clam up."

Susan nods. "It's something you learn. Years ago, I was like you, I wouldn't open my mouth around strangers."

"I think it has to do with the way we are brought up. Robin comes from a home where things were discussed, where important guests came in and out of the house. My parents were very unassuming, and only rarely entertained. And they never discussed the future with me, never said anything about a career. I guess they thought I'd get married and have kids, like they did."

"Well, I hope you two have fun," Susan says, if not convincingly. "Why the Bahamas?"

"Because Robin likes it, she's been there before." Maggie searches Susan's face. "I have a feeling you disapprove."

"Not at all. I just think that when you travel and share a room with someone, it helps if you're close."

"We're close enough. Fundamentally, she's all right, we get along. I like myself when I'm with her. She is so contemporary," Maggie says with a heartfelt sigh, and Susan laughs. "No, I mean it. She reads all the right magazines and she's right there in the thick of things. I feel like I don't belong in my own generation, it's all a big lie. They tell women to go ahead and have careers, but when you look around you, or read girls', women's, magazines, it's all about makeup and how to catch a man. It's all so confusing, you don't know what to believe."

"You'll be fine," Susan says and glances at her watch. "It's getting late," she says and starts to clear the table. Maggie rises, too, and places her plate and glass on the counter. No dishwasher, she notes. She walks over to the couch and lies down. She feels pleasantly warm and snug, taken care of. She can hear Susan move around, putting things away, then Susan begins to talk about a neighbor of hers, a woman named Rose, who committed suicide a few years ago, jumping out of her window and hanging from a sheet she had tied to a fixture in the ceiling. She wanted to share her pain with everyone, Susan says. Or, in her craziest moment, Rose had the presence of mind to plan it so that her corpse wouldn't go undiscovered for too long.

What an awful story, Maggie thinks. She can see the body lightly swinging outside the window, an image she thinks she remembers from a black-and-white movie from the fifties. People tell the strangest stories, at the strangest moments, for the strangest reasons.

"You're falling asleep," Susan says, and Maggie opens her eyes; Susan, smiling, is standing over her. "Do you want to sleep over?"

"No, thanks." Maggie sits up. "I want to go home."

"Are you sure?" Susan asks, and Maggie nods. "I'd better go down with you and put you in a cab, make sure you get home safe."

"You're so good to me." The words fly out of Maggie's mouth, and she is momentarily embarrassed. "I mean, you're decent, and sweet. I mean, you're a good friend."

"So are you, honey." Susan touches her hand to Maggie's cheek. "You should give yourself more credit, Maggie. You must believe in yourself."

"I know," Maggie says, suddenly reluctant to leave this warm, pleasant nest. "I try to, really, I do my best, I think I'm getting there."

FOUR MORE DAYS, AND SHE'LL BE LEAVING this dump. No, not a dump— Maggie looks around her, regretting her thought. When she comes back from Paradise, she'll have to fix up this place. Every space has its potential. Her studio measures five hundred square feet, and she has two windows, facing south and west. She is not crazy about the neighborhood—she's on Fifth Street, between A and B—but everybody says the East Village is the place to be. She agrees, but wishes she were a little more to the west, a little more to the north, say Broadway and Ninth Street.

Weekends, if it's not snowing, she goes jogging in Tompkins Square Park, a five-minute walk from her apartment. It is Saturday morning, and it's not snowing, so Maggie puts on her sneakers, her sports bra, a couple of layers, a hat, stuffs her keys in her pocket and walks out. It's eight o'clock in the morning, and the streets of her neighborhood are quite deserted. A couple of homeless men huddle together on a bench, covered in blankets. Imagining germs swarming all around them, Maggie stops breathing for a couple of seconds and walks fast, past the bench and its human cargo. She is fearful and determined at the same time. Fearful that at this early weekend hour some deranged wino will attack her with a knife. Determined to live her life, regardless.

She reaches the park, jogs for twenty minutes and works up a sweat. There are several other joggers, walkers, a few dogs and their owners. Later, the parents will arrive with their toddlers. These new parents are young and hip, perhaps a touch too smug and know-it-all. Maggie imagines that the kids will grow up to be even worse than their progenitors, doubly smug and obnoxious. But she likes the punks and druggies, wrapped in their blankets on the grass, eating a breakfast of donuts. She feels attracted to them, to their exotic, open-ended lives.

She stretches out on a bench and breathes deeply, her fingertips resting at her rib-cage cavity, monitoring the movement of her diaphragm. She keeps her eyes open and looks at the sky, then shuts them, almost drifting back to sleep. When she decides it's time, she stands up and begins to head back, going past The Turtle Bar. Curiosity propels her to peek inside through the open door. Often, as she goes past, she glimpses the dim interior, the few, mostly old, men already stooped over the bar, drinking. It always amazes her that at such an early hour there would be people drinking. This morning, she feels a strong urge to go inside and join them, live a different life if only for a day. She'll sit at the bar, order beer after beer until she's good and drunk. She's never done such a thing before, but would love to try it—a welcome reprieve from her usual routine. She'll sit there with the others and shed all her worries and live the moment. After all, nothing awaits her upstairs, just another Saturday, the dishes, a couple of books, the newspaper.

Yet, she lacks the courage, is unwilling to abuse her body, fill her stomach with beer, her lungs with smoke. In the afternoon, she'll go shopping for a bathing suit and agonize in front of the mirror until she finds just the right one. She may go see a movie, which will bring her closer to dinner-time and more movies on TV. As much as she hates her job, at times the weekends feel empty, meaningless. It is no wonder, she decides, that people have kids. It gives them something to do, someone to love; they create their own love-images.

Later in the day, she goes downstairs to drop a couple of paid bills in the mail box. She risks a red light and runs across the street, braving the rush of oncoming traffic. Coolly, she contemplates the possibility that she is run over by a car. Everything upstairs is left unattended, until they identify her. An easy matter if she's struck down before she drops the envelopes. But, if struck on her way back, all they could surmise (from her clothing: sweat pants, jacket, sneakers, keys, no pocketbook) is that she lives in the neighborhood. It will take them a while to find out who she is, at which time they will use her own keys—found near her body and perhaps bloody—and go into the apartment, find the soup (leek and potato) simmering on a low flame on the stove, several pairs of underwear soaking in soapy water in the bathroom sink. It's a likely scenario, made all the more nauseating in view of the fact that she didn't have to go out just now, didn't have to make this special trip to the mail box. If she hadn't gone down, she would still be alive.

But she is still alive!—she is almost giddy with relief. She has dropped the envelopes and now makes her way back, being very cautious crossing the street. And here she is, safe on the other side, walking toward the entrance of her building. A homeless person is hanging about, but she has nothing to fear: one of the handymen is vacuuming the lobby. And the obese mailman is there, too, distributing the mail into the boxes. Everything looks normal, and she is still alive. She wonders if all people who live alone entertain such mirthless thoughts. Robin? Probably not. Susan? Probably yes. Susan who knows women who jump out of windows, hanging from a sheet.

A T HER DESK, MAGGIE SCRIBBLES IN A PAD:

> Know
> don't know
> don't know
> know
> not
> don't know
> don't no
> no yes
> don't no

S HE IS SAYING GOODBYE TO NEW YORK. She walks over to the Korean grocer who always greets her with a smile. "I'm going to the Bahamas," she tells him, and his pallid, moonish face bobs up and down, and he smiles his enigmatic smile.

She's in high spirits, and is a bit disappointed in his bland reaction. Maybe he didn't understand her? "I mean," she continues, "I won't be buying vegetables for a while. You won't see me, I'm saying goodbye."

He nods and smiles again, his hands reaching for the two apples, two bananas, one red pepper she has placed on the counter. It is painfully, embarrassingly obvious she shops for one person only, but he already knows this about her.

"I'm leaving the day after tomorrow, that's why I'm buying so little. I have to plan my shopping so that nothing is left to rot in my refrigerator."

"Sure, sure," says the grocer, punching numbers on his machine. "One-sixty-eight," he tells her, and she looks in her purse for the exact change. It's a good opportunity to get rid of her pennies and loose change. There's no one on line who might be annoyed with her for taking up so much time. She herself is easily annoyed with those who search for pennies and hold up the line. She looks at them and thinks, How petty-minded they are, so careful with their money, so miserly. Then feels guilty for being so unforgiving, so quick to judge.

Here, she has counted out the exact change.

"Have good time," says the grocer, and she thanks him and leaves the store. Have good time, yes, and *hasta la vista*. When she gets upstairs, maybe she'll call Robin, just to chat a little. She feels good tonight, despite the weather, despite Mr. Faber. Mr. Faber who's been more sullen today than usual. Maybe he begrudges her vacation, her getting away.

Why do people like Faber exist in the world? Robin says that Maggie is naive and not assertive enough, and Robin must be right. Get real, Robin says, only confusing Maggie more. She is not stupid, thank God; at times she even feels intelligent. But obviously, she is missing the point. In some fundamental way she lacks the necessary knowledge or information. She could blame her parents, of course, especially her father, but what's the use? She should call him before she leaves to say goodbye, and maybe she will, tomorrow, from the office. If she feels up to it.

Upstairs, she dials Robin's number, speaks to Robin's machine, hoping that Robin will pick up. She doesn't. Maybe she's not home, although sometimes, when Maggie talks to the machine, she has a distinct, uneasy feeling that Robin is there, listening. Answering machines are sinister. No, her thoughts are. Robin's probably out, having dinner with friends from CBS. Those friends from CBS inhabit a different world. Could she fit in that world? Yes, she could. It would take some time and patience on her part, but given the opportunity she could demonstrate her true worth. For she does have good qualities, loyalty being one of them, a scarce commodity in that world. She won't say much at first, but will listen, absorb a lot and, like a sponge, will grow fuller, smarter. Given the opportunity.

A T LAST, TIME TO PACK. MAGGIE SELECTS from the closet the items of clothing she'll take with her and tosses them all on the bed. She gets two shoulder bags, one large, one smaller, and carefully, lovingly, folds each garment and fits it in a bag. Humming, she congratulates herself for having decided to go. Had she said no to Robin and Paradise, she'd be adding yet another ordinary night to the tally of her life, consuming yet another lonely dinner while watching TV. By saying yes to Robin, she has opened the door to a whole new set of possibilities. She puts on her new bathing suit and inspects the front and back in the mirror. She draws in her breath and moves her hand up and down the cold lycra fabric, adhering so lustily to her flattened stomach.

She looks around her: everything is ready. She checks an urge to call Robin and scream for joy; she'd better learn to be as cool and self-possessed as Robin. Being cool is the thing. She lights a joint and turns on her stereo and, after a moment's deliberation, puts on *Rigoletto* with Callas and Tito Gobbi. She always cries listening to it, and if she cries tonight her eyes will be puffy in the morning. She knows this, but can't help herself; she is in the mood.

Eyes shut, sitting cross-legged on the couch, she sways with the music. Here they come, the tears. She can still stop, turn off the music, wash her face. But no, she can't stop, it's too beautiful. The way they sing to each other, father and daughter. It could be her father singing to her, but her father doesn't care for opera, or much else that she knows of.

A fresh burst of tears—she sobs into the tissue. A good cry before leaving will do her good. Even if her eyes are puffy in the morning. A small price to pay, ridding herself of excess baggage. Excess baggage. Pack light, Robin said, and she did. When she comes home from the trip, she may come back a whole new person, facing a whole new future. It is so tempting to let routine and dark thoughts rule your life, but she, she took the initiative and said yes to change.

T HEY'RE IN THE BACK SEAT OF A BLACK, car-service sedan, and they're on their way. Maggie can barely contain her excitement. She wants to share it with Robin, but Robin seems cranky and aloof at this hour of the morning.

"Say goodbye to the snow, Robin," Maggie says softly.

"Yes." Robin lets out a sigh and looks out the window.

"You were so smart to suggest that we go away," Maggie continues. "It's so wonderful not to have to think about your life."

"Please, Maggie, you're too cheerful." Robin leans back against the cushions and shuts her eyes. "Wake me up when we get there."

Secretly, Maggie scrutinizes her friend: the full, pouting mouth, the small ears, the abundant, reddish hair, the very fair skin. Not for the first time, Maggie searches Robin's face, trying to grasp the source of her friend's appeal, the source of her hold over others, friends and strangers alike. The wealthy, Maggie reflects, have this sure manner about them, and this is what attracts others. Money is more than money, and if you're blessed with both money and looks it is naturally assumed that it is old money, that good genes have been in the family for generations. Robin never takes a shower—only baths. She oozes the voluptuousness of candy, of white

Belgian chocolate. Looking at Robin, Maggie reflects, your mouth comes alive: you remember your lips, your tongue, the function of your teeth.

Yet Robin, Maggie notes with a touch of satisfaction, is on the plump side; she must watch what she eats, is constantly on and off diets. Already Maggie can see the ominous beginning of a double chin. She can see Robin in twenty years, an overweight, middle-aged woman, with only faint traces of beauty to remind her of her youth.

Maggie contemplates Robin's hands: they're sort of small and chubby, like a spoiled child's, the fingernails painted bright red. Maggie hates nail polish, never bothers with the stuff. She thinks it makes women look older, giving them a tidy, pinched look, which Maggie finds unattractive. But most men, it seems, go for women who wear nail polish, women who devote time to the way they look, women who know how to fix themselves up. For her part, Maggie hopes there's a man out there who would want her just the way she is, natural, without excessive primping and artifice.

Maggie glances at the young, Middle-Eastern-looking driver, then turns to the window, leans her elbow on the armrest. She considers asking him how long he's been in this country, but Robin may not appreciate this over-friendliness toward a driver. They're heading up First Avenue to the Midtown Tunnel. Maggie is tempted to lean back and, like Robin, shut her eyes, but decides, No. She wants to be awake every minute of her vacation.

She looks over at Robin, still resting against the cushions. It was wrong of her to delight in Robin's double chin. Robin is her friend. Soon they'll be on the island, relaxing on the beach, strolling in the casino. They'll meet people, fuck their brains out.

Fuck their brains out—Maggie smiles. But what exactly

does it mean? Is the guy so big, he reaches your brain? Do you become unconscious? Is your brain so filled with sex, you plunge into blissful oblivion? And most important: How do you unfuck your brain, once it's fucked?

She could ask Robin, but Robin is asleep, or feigning sleep. It's cold and white outside; mountains of snow embank the sidewalk. The other day, walking out of the public library on Fifth Avenue, carrying books for the trip, she noticed a man, a lame dwarf, right ahead of her, swinging on his crutches. God, she thought. How does he manage in this awful weather? Her heart went out to him, filled with compassion for his small frame, his threadbare shoes and nothing jacket, when the dwarf suddenly burst into song, singing some Spanish love lyric in this rich, baritone voice, and she followed behind, marvelling at the thought that even this dwarf, for all his wretched appearance, is happy, is equipped for happiness, a thought that filled her with hope and gratitude.

They're on the Expressway now, and the hum of the engine, and the industrial towers dotting the bare landscape, thrill her. She imagines herself in the huge casino, hears the jingling music of the slot machines, and is thrust into a high gear of expectation. She may get lucky, win a bundle. She has gone a couple of times to Atlantic City with Robin, has learned to like roulette, blackjack, craps. In the casino, cash is the great equalizer. If you gamble, you're in: gender, age, looks, make no difference. And most gamblers are friendly, out to have a good time. She particularly likes the roulette tables, is especially intrigued by the females, the high rollers among them, who lose or win hundreds without a blink of an eye. She spies on them, evaluates the rings, the bracelets, the fine cut and fabric of their expensive outfits—they, obviously, can easily carry their losses. They keep a blank, distant expression on their immaculate, made-up faces. What brings them here, she wonders. Why do they need to win—they have so much money already. Her situation is laughably different. When she goes into a casino she hopes to supplement her income, hopes to win fifty, or a hundred, and so far has managed to realize a small win on almost every trip. Usually twenty, or thirty bucks. Hope is the name of the game, and she likes hope, is good at it.

They arrive at the airport, and the driver puts their luggage on a porter's cart. Robin, Maggie notices, has packed a suit bag.

"Why a suit bag?" she asks as they follow the porter into the terminal.

Robin looks at her. "Well, what does it look like, Maggie? I brought a couple of dressy outfits."

"What for?" Maggie persists, then seeing the expression on Robin's face, quickly adds, "You're on vacation."

"Well," Robin says, "I just felt like it."

"But you said," Maggie murmurs. "I packed only casuals."

"Good." Robin tosses her handbag on the cart. "You look better in casuals."

At the information desk, they are directed upstairs to gate twenty-nine. Twenty-nine, Maggie notes, is a good number. She should play it today when she hits the tables.

They get their boarding passes, and now there's nothing more to do, but wait to board the plane. Maggie looks around her, observes the other travellers, their carry-on luggage. Like her, they've gladly put their lives on hold and now look forward to a great vacation.

I love airports, she wants to tell Robin. I love the feeling of suspension, of anticipation. I like flying, I even like the food—I like to be fed.

Will they serve breakfast on the plane? she wonders. She can feel the pull in her stomach, the beginning of hunger.

"I wish we were there already," Robin mutters. "I have no patience for this."

"Yeah," Maggie says. She wishes Robin were in a better mood. "Do you think they'll serve breakfast?"

"That's all you think about? Food?" Robin mocks.

"I'm hungry," Maggie retorts, raising her voice. If Robin is on a diet, it doesn't mean that she, too, has to starve. "What's bugging you?"

"Of course they'll serve breakfast," Robin says in a subdued voice, and Maggie feels somewhat triumphant, but also a bit uneasy for having caused this change in Robin. "They always do."

"Well, I wasn't sure. It's a short flight. Would you mind," Maggie asks. "I mean, do you care which seat....? Would you mind if I took the window seat?"

For a long moment, Robin studies her, and Maggie marvels at the translucent clarity of Robin's hazel eyes.

"You're such a baby, Maggie," Robin finally says, and Maggie smiles. She likes it when Robin calls her a baby. She likes it when Robin assumes an authoritative tone, treating Maggie as a child.

"Thank you," Maggie says. "I knew you wouldn't mind."

"You're so shrewd, little Maggie." Robin, smiling, shakes her head. "You always get what you want."

"Not true," Maggie says, but not assertively; she is willing to concede that every now and then she gets what she wants.

Finally in her seat, she quickly establishes her zone of comfort for the next couple of hours: blanket and pillow, just in case. Large bag in the overhead compartment, small bag under the seat before her. She is quite ecstatic, pulls off her sneakers, sits cross-legged—she is ready, all set to go. Right outside the window, she can see the wing—massive, majestic, and ominous. But, she reminds herself, all inanimate objects become ominous if you gaze at them long enough.

Now the plane is in motion, and over the public address system their captain speaks to them: they're ready for takeoff. It's a calm, reassuring voice that is meant to convey they have nothing to worry about, they're in good hands; all a passenger need do is sit back and enjoy. She's a bit nervous, but the thrill she feels is much greater, a thrill compounded by the prospect of danger.

They taxi for a while, and Maggie envisions the huge, heavy machine, clumsily maneuvering into position. A dramatic pause, and then the engines gather power, and here they go, speeding down the runway. Maggie feels her heart expand. She waits for that magical moment when the wheels will leave the ground, and then, all at once, they'll be airborne, defying gravity, and now they are, and she looks outside the window, greedily watches the receding landscape. The plane, gracefully, dips to the left, to the right, and then straightens out.

She takes a deep breath. Over the public address system a flight attendant identifies herself as Sandy and goes over the emergency procedures. Maggie half listens, while taking leave of the landscape below. "...Anyone with a child, or anyone behaving like a child..." Sandy says, and Maggie laughs merrily with all the other passengers. She turns to Robin, but Robin only makes a face.

"Don't you think it's funny?" Maggie asks.

"Very funny." Robin twists her mouth. "Spontaneous wit they repeat on every flight."

"...Passengers found smoking in the lavatory," Sandy continues, "will be asked to leave this aircraft immediately."

At this, everybody explodes, and even Robin smiles, if reluctantly. "They're trained to be funny," she snorts. "Someone writes these lines for them."

"I don't care." Maggie lets an edge creep into her voice. "As long as it's funny."

Soon, Sandy says, they'll serve a light breakfast.

Light breakfast? Maggie begins to worry. She is hungry; she needs more than a light breakfast.

"What do you think they mean by light?" She turns to Robin. "I hope they mean more than just a frozen roll, or a mini-Danish."

"Oh, stop already," Robin mutters and stands up. She pulls open the overhead compartment, shuts it, then glances toward the back of the plane.

She spotted someone, Maggie thinks, suppressing an urge to turn around, to see who it might be. She knows the flicker that comes into Robin's eyes when she notices something she might want to possess.

"Where is he?" Maggie asks as Robin sits down.

"Who?"

Maggie smiles. "The guy. You can't fool me."

"You're impossible, you know that?" Robin says, and Maggie, surprised by the sharp tone, stares at her. Why is Robin so irritable? Robin who's never secretive when it comes to men.

"Take it easy," Maggie says. "I meant nothing by it. What's eating you this morning?"

"Nothing."

"What were you looking for in the overhead compartment?"

"My stupid book, that's what. I thought I'd packed it in my bag."

"I'll lend you one of mine," Maggie says, soothingly. "I've

brought a couple. And a couple of magazines."

"Thanks," Robin says, her eyes large and pensive. "Unless," she says, bends over, pulls up her backpack from under the seat in front of her. It's a Prada, naturally, and Maggie eyes it with mixed emotions. It's a nice enough bag, but she'd never spend so much money on a bag, and certainly not on one that has become a signature.

"Thank God," Robin says. "It's here."

"Good," Maggie says, although she couldn't care less. It's only a book, for crying out loud, she wants to say. Besides, she hasn't known Robin to be such an avid reader. She leans back in her seat. Of course, she, too, could play Robin's little games. She could pretend to be tired, pretend to be asleep throughout the flight. She could be cranky, snooty, short-tempered. Who does Robin think she is? What gives her the right to behave this way?

Her own acquiescence, Maggie has to admit. She herself allows it, it's been this way from the start. Relationships coagulate and settle into patterns not amenable to change. Were Maggie to break from her mold and tell Robin to go fuck herself, Robin would drop dead from the shock.

At the aisle across, a black woman is knitting; how soothing it is to look at her. She is young and pregnant, perhaps a Bahamian travelling back home. Her husband is asleep, his head on her shoulder. How strong she seems, Maggie reflects. So solid. Supporting her husband's head and calmly knitting, carrying a baby in her womb; she is, no doubt, the center of this small unit, this small family-to-be.

"What are you thinking about?" Robin asks.

It works—Maggie notes with disdain. Ignore Robin for a moment, and instantly her inquisitiveness, her need to control, is roused.

"This couple," Maggie replies.

Robin glances their way. "What about them?"

"Nothing. I just like the way they look. She is pregnant."

Robin nods. "You're right, they make a nice picture. Did you bring a camera?"

"No. Did you?"

"I should have. Well, we'll do without." Robin smiles her lovely smile. "Here they come with the trays. Your little greedy tummy will be happy."

"How about yours?"

"I'm not very hungry, but maybe I'll eat something."

Breakfast is surprisingly satisfying: an omelette, a mini-bagel with cream cheese, even a slice of cheap lox. Robin only nibbles at her food, makes a mess of it, spilling coffee onto her plate. Which is a pity: Maggie could have eaten Robin's bagel and lox.

After the trays are collected, Maggie says she needs to go. She makes her way down the aisle, scanning the seats, looking for the guy Robin has spotted. Some heads are raised as she goes past, and she feigns indifference, yet hopes that those who look up find her attractive. It's always been her problem, feigning indifference. Robin, on the other hand, meets someone's gaze straight on.

She reaches the end of the cabin, turns the VACANT knob on one of the doors and enters the small lavatory. She slides the bolt into locking position, and a small florescent tube above her head flickers into light. She doesn't need to pee, but will have to kill time before going back to her seat. Coming down the aisle, she didn't see him, the guy who might be Robin's type. Perhaps she was wrong; Robin did look for her book, after all.

She wipes the seat with tissue paper and sits down. It feels weird to sit down on the toilet with your pants on, but people, she reasons, do weird things, have weird thoughts, when alone and sheltered as she is now. She likes the narrow confines, the compact efficiency, designed to accommodate a passenger's needs.

She leans back and shuts her eyes. As a matter of fact, she feels very comfortable—she could stay right here for the duration of the flight. It's been a tiring morning, trying to humor Robin.

When she gets back to her seat, Robin is reading her book.

"What took you so long?" Robin asks but continues to read, not waiting for a reply. Maggie retrieves her magazine, the current issue of *The New Yorker*, and tries to read, too. She feels restless, her thoughts wander. Maybe she should talk to Robin, see if her mood is improved.

"What are you reading?" she asks.

"Not your kind of book," Robin says and shows her the cover. It's some kind of thriller, and the embossed, glossy picture depicts a woman holding a gun to a man's head. The man is on his knees, evidently begging for his life. How can Robin read such garbage? Maggie thinks. She wouldn't be caught dead with such a book in her hands.

"Is it good?" Maggie asks.

"It's all right."

"You were a bit snippy this morning," Maggie suggests cautiously.

Robin shrugs. "It'll pass."

"I thought it was something I said or did. I thought that maybe you regret having asked me to come."

"Don't be silly. It's not you, it's me," Robin says, and Maggie feels a surge of love for Robin. She wants to love Robin always, she wants Robin to love her back. Everything is so much simpler when she can trust Robin.

"You know," Maggie says. "Susan, my friend at work,

asked if you and I are close. She said that if we are to spend twenty-four hours a day—"

Robin laughs. "Of course we're close. Besides, we won't be together all the time; you'll do your thing, I'll do mine."

"Yes," Maggie says. "I know." She doesn't like the idea of Robin doing her thing, whatever it is, excluding Maggie, but she'd better not say it. "You mean, if we each meet a guy?"

"Yeah," Robin says, "or whatever. We're not Siamese twins, you know. You like to swim, I like to gamble, stuff like that."

"I like to gamble, too. And we'll have our meals together, won't we?"

"I don't know, Mag, why do we have to plan everything now? We'll play it by ear, all right? You know how I am about food." Robin shuts her book and turns to face her. "You think too much ahead, girl. Once we get there, you won't need me, I promise. You'll be having too much fun."

"I will?"

"Of course. That's why we're going, remember? To have fun. Nothing more, nothing less."

"You're right," Maggie says. "I'd better loosen up."

"Exactly, my pet."

Maggie laughs. "I like it when you call me my pet."

Robin smiles. "I know, sweetie, that's why I do it."

THEY LAND IN NASSAU, AND MAGGIE lifts her face to the tropical sun, welcomes its warmth. She looks around her, takes a moment to adjust to the bright sunshine. She's in paradise, she's left New York behind. How tall and serene the trees look, and the blue blue sky—not a cloud in sight. Oh, yes, she thinks. Just let me live. Live. Their package includes ground transportation, and they mount the van that will take them to Paradise Island. Soon, the van fills up with other vacationers, mostly elderly couples, and they're on their way.

Maggie is thrilled. "We're going to Paradise," she tells Robin. The driver, a corpulent native, begins to talk into a microphone, and Maggie listens intently, not wishing to miss a word. The real tourist, she mocks herself, but not too severely.

The driver is funny, he makes them laugh; magically, he transforms a few strangers into one, cohesive group: he's a professional. "I'm taking you," he says, "to eleven-hundred rooms of luxury and fun." Proudly he announces that Sean Connery and Bill Cosby live on the island, and an apprecia-tive murmur fills the van. "In our hotel," the driver intones in his deep, base voice, "you're going to spend some memo-rable days, and"—he adds with a roaring laughter—"NIGHTS!"

Oh, God, Maggie thinks. Nights, yes. She thinks it a good omen that their first moments on the island should be so pleasurable. She leans toward Robin, whispers, "I packed a couple of joints."

"Good." Robin nods.

The driver points their attention to a pink hotel across the water. He tells them they must come back at night when the hotel is lit up and the sight is just out of this world. We will, Maggie resolves, makes a mental note.

When the van pulls up in front of the hotel, Maggie looks on, as if enchanted. Bell boys in white uniforms and khaki safari helmets stand in formation outside the sliding doors. Like a picture postcard, she thinks, or a movie scene shot in colonial Africa.

"Run inside and post yourself on a check-in line," Robin commands. "I'll take care of the bags."

"Right," Maggie says, full of admiration for Robin's ingenuity. "Don't forget to tip him," she whispers, motioning the driver.

"Go," Robin says.

Almost panicky, she runs into the lobby, determined to get on the shortest line. This one. No, that one. She'd better make up her mind, before more people arrive. This one, she decides. There are only a couple of people in front of her, but already she is seething with impatience. She wants to be upstairs, in their beautiful room, all unpacked and settled, already informed about the hotel, the island, the ins and outs. Then she could start her vacation. She would open a door into the moment and step inside.

She turns on her heels, hopes to see Robin come in through the doors. The lobby is spacious and colorful: a sparkling marble floor, potted palm trees, wicker chairs. A few people lounge about, clad in typical resort wear. Against the bright sun outside, the lobby becomes a cool, shaded oasis. Robin is nowhere in sight.

Where is she? Maggie thinks and, for diversion, begins to exercise her glutes. She pushes up on her toes, lands back on her heels. Yes, she is limber, and she delights in it. She turns back to face the counter. The female clerks are so *slow*, so chatty, she could scream. Come on, she urges mutely. Get going, girls. I haven't come all this way to stand on line.

"Easy does it," she hears a soft male voice come from

behind her and, thrilled by the possibility that the voice might belong to just the right person, she gaily swivels on her heels to see who it is. Disappointment. An elderly couple, vouchers in hand, luggage at their feet. Retirees. Neat, organized, determinedly patient.

"I know," she says. More words bubble up in her. "I hate waiting, I have to keep moving. I come from New York," she adds, laughing, but the expression on their faces tells her they don't get it, her special brand of humor; they must think she is odd.

To save face, she gives them a bright smile, then slowly turns to face the counter.

All right, all right, she tells herself. One more minute or less won't make a difference. Not a huge difference. Her vacation will start soon enough. It is good that the clerks are friendly, unhurried. When her turn comes, she, too, will be asking all sorts of questions, oblivious of those others still waiting on line. Patience, little girl, patience.

Yes, patience, tolerance. She must accept that others exist as much as she does.

She looks once more toward the doors. Robin—at last—is entering the lobby. Robin, too, can be excruciatingly slow, but she does use her brains, doesn't she? The way she cleverly thought ahead and sent Maggie to stand on line, while she took care of their luggage. Good thinking, Robin, good thinking. Robin has taken off her jacket, and now looks sharp and sexy in her black, spaghetti-strapped T-shirt. She walks slowly, deliberately, inviting glances as she takes in the lobby. A bell boy has their luggage on a cart.

"Good timing," she calls to Robin, for now it is their turn to check in. "I love this island already," she gushes, loud enough for the clerk to hear. She knows she is being coy, cute, even conniving; she hates this behavior in others, and in herself, yet does it all the same. Why can't she *learn* to control herself?

At the counter, she lets Robin do the talking—Robin can sweet-talk anybody: she'll get the best room, the best view, the best service. Maggie luxuriates in shedding responsibility and leaning against the counter, scrutinizing the clerk. She notes the very dark skin, the long, polished nails, the olive-green uniform. Black men, she reflects, are attracted first and foremost to black women. Often, walking in the city, she notices how black men, instinctively, glance at passing black women, while totally ignoring, not even seeing, Maggie.

"Two beds, please," Robin says.

The clerk smiles. "It's noted in the voucher."

"How efficient," Robin says, perhaps condescendingly, and Maggie searches the clerk's face for signs of annoyance, but finds none. Perhaps she reads too much into Robin's manner.

The clerk hands them keys, wishing them a pleasant stay. "Let the fun begin," Maggie cries as they walk to the elevators, and Robin says, "Cool it, Mag."

Upstairs, they unlock the door and walk in. "Wow," Maggie says, taking in the room and walking straight to the glass doors of the veranda. Beyond the palm and banana trees, she can see a sliver of ocean, sharp and smooth as a blade, glinting in the bright sun. She loves the deep-green leaves of the banana trees. They're so thick and heavy, they look unreal, as if made of plastic. She is vaguely aware of Robin moving in the room, but is reluctant to turn around. All at once she is worried. She and Robin have shared a room before, but never for more than one night; what if they quarrel?

No, they won't, they're in paradise!

Maggie smiles and turns to face the room, the two double beds, the wide mirror, the commode. She loves the soothing, pastel colors, the white and peach motif of the walls and bedspreads.

"Come on, let's unpack," Robin says. "Which bed do you want?"

"This one, if you don't mind." Maggie, grateful that Robin lets her choose, points at the bed nearest the glass doors. Already she imagines how, in the evenings, before they go to dinner, they'll sit on the veranda, watch the sunset and sip a drink, smoke a cigarette.

They unpack their bags, and divide the counter space in the bathroom, the hangers in the closet.

"Hurry up, I'm starved," Robin says and begins to undress.

"Starved? It's too early for lunch."

"Who cares? I haven't eaten breakfast, remember?"

Well, you should have, Maggie wants to say, but that's not a good way to start a vacation. "All right," she says and sits down on her bed. She begins to sort out the creams and lotions in her cosmetics bag. She'd rather go straight to the beach, plunge into the cool water, but they're two on this trip, they'll have to accommodate one another.

As she busies herself with her creams and lotions, she glimpses Robin as Robin unhooks her black, strapless bra, pulls down her underwear. She has seen Robin in various stages of undress, but never managed a good look. She sneaks another glance, scanning Robin's round, heavy breasts, her pink nipples, her fine pubic hair. There's something secret, Maggie reflects, possibly obscene, in a woman's naked flesh. Having to do, perhaps, with the long-established, deeply ingrained concepts of mother and whore. Robin's vagina, she notes, is plump and fleshy, sprawling on its mound. Hers, in comparison, is perhaps more elegant: flat and narrow, it stretches toward her anus.

Robin gets into her tiny white bikini, and Maggie stands up and begins to undress, wondering if Robin scrutinizes her as she does Robin. Probably not, she concludes. Robin is too self-absorbed to pay real attention.

Maggie pulls on her new black swimsuit, grabs a long print shirt, and they leave the room, walk down the hall toward the elevators; Maggie wants to skip and twirl like a girl.

"I can't believe we're here," she says and hits the down button. Robin, seemingly willing to indulge Maggie, gives her a small, forgiving smile.

Exuberant, Maggie trills, "Paradise, I'm in Paradise."

"Yes, you are," Robin says. "Just remember who brought you here."

H OW GOOD SHE FEELS IN THE WATER! She is graceful, like a fish, like a blue whale, mastering the vast expanse of water. She twists and turns, flips over. On her back, on her stomach, on her side. The gentle breeze forms tiny waves and bubbles across the surface, and as she swims with the current, she feels that her body, long and trim, swiftly crosses the ocean, cuts through the water like a kayak, light and brisk. She adopts the serenity of an accomplished swimmer, imagines she competes in the Olympics. If nothing else, she'll swim her brains out. She could swim forever, oh yes, she could, never tire of the steady, rhythmic motion. How fortunate she is to be here.

Very few people are in the water. She shades her eyes, looks out to the shore. She locates Robin under the yellow beach umbrella, but cannot tell whether Robin is reading or is dozing off. Robin, to protect her white skin, hides from the sun and avoids the water. Earlier, they sat at the snack bar near the pool, shared an order of fried conch, and had two Bahama Mamas each, a pink drink that Robin said was the best thing on the island. In her lazy, flirtatious manner, Robin asked the man behind the counter why the drink is called Bahama Mama. The man, who up to that point had been aloof and unfriendly, suddenly smiled at Robin, then stood there, pondering her question. "I don't know," he finally said. "Nobody ever asked me this question before. It's just a name, I think." He prepared them another drink, on the house, and again Maggie marvelled at Robin's talent to disarm just anyone. She, too, she thought, should try it, be amiable, ask questions, make contact with strangers.

After lunch, Robin preferred to remain at the pool, but agreed to accompany Maggie down to the beach, even if Maggie had to beg. She hates to arrive somewhere all alone, she feels self-conscious, certain that everybody, perhaps out of boredom, is watching her with critical, investigating eyes.

How clumsy she feels on land, how comfortable, unencumbered, she feels in the water. She must have been a dolphin in a previous life.

Maggie dives under water, then swims some more. She'll swim for a half hour, then come out and collapse on the sand. She'll read for a while, or chat with Robin. Depending on Robin's mood.

Blue, blue everywhere. Quiet, peaceful. She loves Robin, Robin who patiently waits on the beach. In this calm, she finds it easy to suspend all judgment. She herself is suspended, her legs, like a mermaid's, in constant motion, keep her afloat. She tilts sideways, observes her firm thighs, her muscular calves, long and slender in the water, long and slender in their slow, graceful motion. She is a nymph, all alone in the deep.

She shades her eyes, looks out to shore. She locates the yellow umbrella, spots the reddish head. She thinks she sees another person under the umbrella, his back turned to the water. Yes, definitely. The wide, tan back of a man, under Robin's umbrella.

Maggie's heart begins to pound as she swims in. Her arms feel heavy, and she tells herself to calm down, what's the hurry? As a matter of fact, it may be better if she takes her time and stays longer in the water, and so allow Robin to do her thing.

But what if, Maggie thinks. What if Robin and the guy hit it off—where does it leave her? Will she have to, for the next few days and nights, keep out of their way?

She comes out of the water, shakes out her hair, slowly walks toward the umbrella, toward the tan back of the guy seated on a towel at Robin's feet. Does a man's mind fasten on a woman, not to let go? Or can he change his mind once he sees her girlfriend? She smiles at the thought, and keeps a smiling face as she approaches them, bends under the umbrella and reaches for her towel with a happy, friendly, "Hello!"

Robin looks up and smiles; the man turns around to welcome her. He, too, is smiling, and as Robin introduces them, and Maggie extends her hand to him, she concludes, Not bad. Good face, good bone structure, good teeth. Expensive, polarized sunglasses. Nice shoulders and chest. Not too hairy, not too muscular; the guy is just right. If he has half a brain....

"This is Maggie," Robin says in her nonchalant, lingering voice, "and this is Allen. He, too, arrived today."

"Today?" Maggie says incredulously. If it's true, this guy tans fast. But why would he lie? "Boy," she says, before she can stop herself. "You tan fast."

Allen laughs. "My skin loves the sun."

"Allen," Robin says. "There's something you must know about Maggie." Robin smiles at Maggie, and Maggie wonders what Robin is up to now. "You see, Maggie has to know everything, and I do mean *everything*, all the whys and hows and whens. She also has this idea that people never tell the truth. I don't know if it's your common variety of social phobia or something worse."

"Really?" Allen says, smiling at Maggie.

"Absolutely not true," Maggie, also smiling, intones.

"It is, it is," Robin continues. "I never lie."

Stop already, Maggie wants to say, but doesn't.

"Well," Allen tells Maggie. "I go to tanning salons." He searches the pockets of his shirt folded on the towel. "And that's the absolute truth."

"Do you really?" Robin leans forward, closer to him. "I hate those places."

"I'm vain, you see, just like a woman." Allen laughs and lights a cigarette.

"You flew in from New York?" Maggie asks. "On our flight?"

"Well," Allen begins, but Robin cuts him off. "No," she says. "He flew in from Newark."

"From Newark?" Maggie repeats, feeling stupid. Her voice sounds hollow and vacant in her ears. How come she always gets herself into the most inane conversations? "You live in New Jersey?"

"Oh, Maggie," Robin says. "Don't start. What did I tell you?" She turns to Allen.

Maggie knows she must hide her face; she can feel it burning with humiliation. She turns from them and spreads her towel on the sand.

There's an awful, awkward silence, then she hears Allen say, "I don't mind, really. Actually, Maggie—" He reaches for her, and she is eternally relieved and grateful for the attention. "If you really want to know, I live in Brooklyn."

Allen and Robin laugh, and she, still wavering between hurt and forgiveness, hesitates a moment then settles on forgiveness; she smiles at him, screws up her face into that innocent-baffled expression, so dear to men, reputedly. For a magical, intense moment, she and Allen stare at one another.

"Brooklyn," Robin says dreamily, and Allen shifts his gaze to Robin. "Brooklyn is such an ethnic place. Maggie and I never go to Brooklyn. Right, Maggie?"

Reluctantly, obligingly, Maggie nods. Robin is trying to make amends, and she'll relent, if only for the sake of their vacation. Fucking Robin has to appear superior, especially when a good-looking guy is in the vicinity. She'll let Robin get away with it, but just this once.

"Where in Brooklyn?" Robin asks, pushing her painted toes into the sand.

"Park Slope."

"Park Slope is not bad," Robin says, and again Robin and Allen laugh. Robin actually doubles over, buries her gorgeous face between her smooth, impeccable knees.

Maggie watches them, resentment welling up in her. What's so funny? she wonders. And why can't she lighten up and join the laughter? Because she can't. And if she were to ask, "What's so funny?" they'd laugh even harder, wouldn't bother to answer. She is *so* obtuse, their laughter would say.

"What's so funny?" she asks in a controlled voice. From the look on their faces, you'd think that she was the stranger, not Allen. The two of them are wearing sunglasses; she can't see their eyes.

"What's your problem, Maggie?" Robin asks.

"*My* problem?!" Her voice quavers with restrained exasperation. "I don't have a problem. I just asked—what's so funny." As she says the words, the thought flashes through her mind that Robin and Allen may have smoked a joint; how else explain their bizarre behavior.

"Cool it, sweetie, we're just laughing." Robin moves her hands up and down her calves; her red fingernails glint in the bright light—droplets of blood on the milky skin. "If you don't find it funny, you don't have to laugh. Right, Allen?"

"Right," Allen says, and she hates them both. She considers reaching into her bag and getting her magazine, but decides against such an overt expression of hostility.

"Have you hit the casino?" Allen asks.

"Not yet," says Robin. "Have you?"

"Just for a little while. Cost me three hundred." Allen laughs.

Three hundred! Maggie is awed. Her entire gambling budget.

"What did you play?" she asks, and Allen looks at her as if he didn't expect her to join the conversation.

"Roulette," he says.

"I love roulette," Maggie says.

"Here's the waiter," Robin says. "Get us a drink, will you, Allen? Maggie, would you like one, too?"

"Yes," she says, guardedly. She is hot and sweaty, would like to hide from the sun, but there's no room for her under the umbrella.

The waiter, a slim boy in a white uniform, comes over.

He holds an empty tray in his hand, and he stands there, stooping deferentially, waiting for their order, gawking at Robin. The poor thing, Maggie thinks. He can't help himself.

"A Bahama Mama for the lady," Allen says dryly. "What will you have?" He turns to Maggie.

"The same," Maggie says, a bit surprised at Allen's new manner, at the tone he employs with the waiter. She wants the same, yes. The same as Robin. Is Allen blind? Can't he see that she is so much better than Robin? More sensitive, more sincere, more truthful and real in her affections? He's only a plaything for Robin, whereas Maggie would offer him the full range of her emotions. Obviously, that's not what he wants. How shallow he is, they both are. If it's a one-night stand he wants, he's made the right choice. Guys, she muses, can tell such things, can tell a one-night flirt like Robin from a committed love prospect like herself. It would be interesting to see who will dump whom first: Robin Allen, or Allen Robin.

"Make it three Bahama Mamas," Allen says, his inflection telling the waiter to beat it. The boy, getting the message, hugs the tray to his chest and hurries off.

Maggie looks at Allen. He has taken off his sunglasses and nakedly stares at Robin. How protective, possessive he is of his catch, his trophy. He is eating Robin up. With his mouth, his eyes, he is eating her up, licking and biting every inch of bare skin, burying his face, his tongue, in the deep line between her breasts. It is arousing for Maggie to just watch Allen watch Robin, to just imagine what goes through his mind. Robin and her tricks. Robin who, in her white bikini and plump flesh, looks so crushingly innocent, so crushingly smart and soft all over.

"How come you know what drink Robin likes?" Maggie asks Allen. She puts a smile on her face.

"Ah," Allen says. "That's for me to know and for you to find out."

"I'm willing," she says, wishing to sound clever, whimsical.

"Willing—what?" Robin asks.

"To find out."

Robin laughs. "I love you, Maggie. You're so unpredictable."

"Really?" An awkward sort of chuckle escapes her throat. She wants to ask Robin in what way she's unpredictable, but decides it's safer not to push her luck.

"She doesn't strike me as unpredictable," Allen says.

"But she is. Trust me on this," Robin tells Allen.

She is tossed between them. Like a ball. She begins to think that she is the one who smoked a joint.

"I trust you," Allen says. "After all, you've known her much longer."

"That's for sure," Robin says. "I've known her for *ages*."

Maggie listens, tries to detect a subtext; if only she knew what they were talking about.

"It is good that you know me," she tells Robin, her voice a bit tense. "I need you to protect me."

"Protect you from what?" Allen asks.

Maggie smiles at him, but won't say. She scrunches up her nose, inviting Allen's guesses, but Allen is now intent on Robin who parts her legs a little and rubs suntan lotion onto her fleshy inner thighs. Allen licks his lips, and Maggie can hear him think: Honey, let me do it for you.

Their drinks arrive. The waiter, trying very hard not to look at Robin, waits to be paid.

Robin sips her drink; Maggie hesitates. Allen, obviously, intends to pay for Robin's drink. Will he pay for hers as well? From the slowness of his movement, from the way he reaches for his wallet and then lingers, she gathers she's expected to pay for herself.

She reaches for her things, says, "Wait. Let me give you some money."

"No, it's all right," Allen murmurs as if too preoccupied to worry about such trifles.

"I insist." She hands the waiter a ten-dollar bill; she can afford to pay for her own drinks.

The tightwad, she thinks. Robin should take notice. Robin who hates guys who are too cautious with their money. She darts a glance at Robin, hoping to see her wince, hoping they might exchange a meaningful smile, but Robin is oblivious.

As Maggie sips her drink, a new thought occurs to her. Perhaps money is not the issue. Toying with her is. And the two of them are in on it. While she was in the water, Robin and Allen somehow have achieved a quick understanding.

She is being paranoid, she tells herself. It makes no sense. Why would they want to toy with her?

Because, she concludes. To amuse themselves. To amuse Robin. To establish a bond between them.

"I hate plastic," she hears Robin say. "Why can't they bring our drinks in normal glasses?"

"Because," Allen says. "They don't allow glass on the beach."

"Why not?"

"Because glass breaks. It can be dangerous."

Maggie listens. How patiently Allen answers Robin's silly questions. She herself would never have such a banal conversation with a man she wants. But Robin is different. This is her way of letting Allen know she wants him to baby her.

"Ah, well." Robin sighs. "Let it be plastic. You know, Allen," Robin changes her tone. "Maggie and I are like two sisters. I can say anything to her, and she can say anything to me. True or false, Mag?"

"True." Maggie is hesitant. Yet she loves it when Robin calls her Mag.

"And she's damn smart, too. Watch out for Maggie." Robin smiles at her. "Mag, come under the umbrella. You've had too much sun already."

"There's no room."

"Of course there is," Allen says, moving closer to Robin—his head is practically between Robin's knees. "Come join us."

Mollified, she hands Allen her drink to hold for her while she spreads her towel near them.

"Much cozier, isn't it?" Robin whispers.

"Yes, much."

"How was the water?" Robin asks.

"Great. I'm so happy to be here." She sighs from the bottom of her heart, looks out at the water. It's like a huge grave, so blue, so peaceful, so inviting. She is filled with a sudden longing, mixed with apprehension. "I should swim at least three times a day. You, too, Robin. Too bad you have to worry about your skin all the time."

"Maggie," Robin tells Allen, "is still deep in her anal phase. She sets up rules about everything she does. True or false, Mag?"

"True." She smiles to show she's taking it all in stride.

"Maggie works for a publisher in the city," Robin continues, "but she hates her job. Her salary is absurd. As soon as I'm established at CBS, I plan to bring her over."

"You are?" Maggie says; it's all news to her.

"You bet," says Robin.

Allen makes a show of glancing at his watch. "Well, girls, I'd better get going." He springs up on his feet.

It's my fault, she thinks. Maggie as subject matter bores him.

Stealthily, she looks up at his thighs, so naked, hairy, and muscular. She glimpses the outline of his penis pushing against the tight trunks. Robin, she imagines, is also watching him, yet Allen seems perfectly at ease. Aren't men, she wonders, self-conscious about their bodies?

"I'll call you later," Allen says. "Or I'll find you in the casino."

"All right," Robin says.

After Allen leaves, Maggie digs her feet into the sand. Left alone with Robin, she suddenly feels empty. Which is odd. Robin is her friend. They came all this way together.

But this business about CBS—is she supposed to be thankful, ask Robin for details?

She won't, she decides. As a matter of fact, she doesn't feel like talking, she still feels a bit hurt; let Robin say the first word, let her apologize.

That's ridiculous, she thinks. Playing games.

She forces out a laugh, says, "I should have stayed in the water. I chased him away."

"Not at all," Robin says. "You heard what he said. He'll call later."

"Call, where?"

"Our room."

"You gave him our room number?"

"Why not?"

"I don't know." Maggie thinks a moment. "I guess you're right. It's not like you've given him your home phone number. Do you like him?" she asks, looks up at Robin. Yes, she is pretty, painfully so. In her naked shoulders, her ponytail, her dark sunglasses, Robin is a knockout.

"I don't know," Robin says, looks out to the water. "Do

you?"

"I think he likes you."

"Well, we'll see." Robin smiles. "We have yet to hit the casino."

"One night," Maggie says, "I'd like us to go to that pink hotel the driver talked about."

"Here you go again, making plans."

"I want to see it, they say it's beautiful."

"We will, sweetie, but must we discuss it? We'll play it by ear, all right?"

"Why did you have to tell him all these hurtful things about me?"

"What things?" Robin seems genuinely surprised.

"That I'm anal, for one."

"But I was teasing, sweetie, I didn't mean it."

"He doesn't know us well enough to know you were teasing. What an awful impression he must have of me."

"Oh," Robin says. "So you do like him."

"That's not the point," Maggie says miserably.

"But it is, don't you see? If you don't like him, who cares what he thinks. Now be a good girl and stop worrying your cute little head." Robin places both her hands on Maggie's shoulders. "Cheer up, that's an order," Robin says, and Maggie laughs.

IN THE EVENING, THEY GO DOWN TO THE casino. Robin is wearing a black Chanel dress, while Maggie is more casual in her off-white linen pants and cotton-knit gray shirt. Just before they left the room, Robin gathered up her hair in a bun, and Maggie wondered why Robin, while on vacation, would choose to convey such a formal, if elegant, look.

"Hoping to catch a millionaire?" Maggie said and laughed, looking at Robin through the mirror, trying to rid herself of residual resentment still loitering in her person.

Robin, thoughtfully, regarded her through the mirror. "Why?" she asked. "Do I look it?"

"You look gorgeous," Maggie said, and Robin smiled at her image, obviously admiring the results of her handiwork.

In the elevator, going down, Robin checks herself in the mirrored wall, and Maggie, needing something to do, examines her own reflection. How drab-looking she seems next to Robin. Her outfit is all wrong, she doesn't stand out, she looks fat, her features sort of blend into the background. The effect of her thoughts is deadening, so she turns to look at Robin to take her mind off herself. Robin says they'll gamble for a while, and then decide about dinner. Allen hasn't called. "So fuck the jerk," Robin says. "There are many other fish in the tank."

"In the tank?"

Robin inclines her head, and her long earrings glitter in the light. Robin's eyes are filled with pity. "Yes, Maggie, the tank. I'm going to get a salt-water tank for my living room, with tropical monsters swimming in it. It's good for your blood pressure."

"I'm sure," Maggie says, slowly. "But what does it have to do with Allen?"

"Who's talking about Allen? We're talking about a fish-tank."

"All right," Maggie says, catching on, "a fish-tank. That's not a bad idea, but you'd have to feed them live fish."

"So?"

"I couldn't do it."

The elevator doors open and they step out.

"You don't know yourself." Robin hooks her arm through Maggie's and leads her toward the casino. "You're much tougher than you pretend."

"I'm glad you think so."

"I'm your friend, sweetie. I don't know why you keep forgetting this."

Robin's skin is pleasantly cool against hers, and this small gesture of hooking arms, suggesting friendship and closeness, instantly lifts her spirits. She does tend to exaggerate matters, seeking malice where none exists. "You're the coolest chick I know," she tells Robin, "and you smell heavenly."

"That's the secret to success," Robin says. "Remind me to give you my eau de cologne. Here we are my dear, in the belly of the beast."

They enter the large floor of the casino, and Maggie feels her heartbeat accelerate. The lights, the people, the various clicks and jingles of the slot machines. The constant humming noise of a living, vibrant thing, indeed a beast. How huge, she reflects, these casinos are. You walk and walk and there's no end in sight. Only people, and more people, and rows upon rows of slot machines and gaming tables. She takes a deep breath, reminding herself she mustn't get carried away; she'd better be conservative, as she normally is in Atlantic City. Conservative with her money. She is not out to make a killing. She's out to have some fun, win a little at a time, in a slow, steady progression.

The casino is crowded, but not too crowded. Robin is leading them toward the roulette tables. They find one with a couple of seats open, and Maggie picks the seat at the center so she can reach all the numbers; Robin takes the other seat at the end of the table—she plays black or red, she doesn't need to reach the numbers.

Heart pounding, Maggie lays down a fifty, asks the croupier for one-dollar chips. Robin lays down a hundred, asks for five-dollar chips. Maggie places the chips on her carefully selected numbers. It's a five-dollar-minimum table, which means she must play at least five chips each spin, but she plays eight in order to cover her very lucky, and her secondary lucky, numbers. There are additional numbers that she favors, but those she'll play only when she's ahead. When she's way ahead, she may even play twenty chips a spin. But tonight she'll exercise restraint, she's on a budget. If she loses her chips in the first hour, she'll have nothing to do the rest of the evening. She has brought only three hundred dollars to gamble with for the entire week, so she must play wisely, make her money last, avoid the cash machines.

She prays, Please, God, let me win, then chides herself for calling on God for such a frivolous request; she'd better reserve Him for more important pleas. She watches the croupier, a tall, thin-lipped man with a British accent, and wills him to roll one of her lucky numbers.

The croupier twirls the small, metal ball against the wooden edge of the roulette, and the ball begins to spin, round and round, in the groove above the numbers. 0, 14, 17, flash by, catching her eye, and she thinks it a good omen—they're among her primary lucky numbers. Robin, she notices, is playing black. Black is fine with her, provided it fell on 17, or 2. Green—the zero and double zero—would be all right, too: she will win eleven dollars—she is playing the "basket" which covers 0, 00, and 2—and Robin will lose only half her bet. But 17 would be better, for she's got it cornered on all four sides—a win of thirty-two bucks. Not bad at all, she'll happily take it, stack up her chips in rows of tens.

The ball falls on 23. All right, she's got one corner covered, it's not a total loss, she'll get back her initial, eight-dollar investment. But Robin loses: 23 is red. The croupier, with both hands, clears all the losing chips off the table, then separates out the chips on 23 and pays the winners. She gets her eight dollars, places them again on her lucky positions. One extra chip she puts between 23 and 26.

She glances at Robin who is lighting a cigarette, and she looks around her, hoping to spot a cocktail waitress. Once she gets her drink, she, too, will light up. She is beginning to feel that rush, the rush of being in the game, of winning. That's why she came here. To win. To be transformed, and to believe that only good things will come her way, obliterating all past losses, hurts, humiliations.

The croupier spins the ball, and bingo! A repeater! Maggie smiles, quickly calculates how many chips she should get; these croupiers, at times, do miscalculate. If it's in her favor, she won't complain, naturally. She should get eight dollars plus seventeen—twenty five! Not bad, not bad. Where is that cocktail waitress?

"Can we have a waitress?" she calls to the pit boss in a high, demanding voice she barely recognizes as her own.

"I'll see what I can do," he says, a response that doesn't please her. Just do it, she thinks, and do it fast.

She is on a roll, nothing and no one can stop her. She is rolling, spinning, playing her numbers, losing all notion of time. This croupier is all right—she tips him a couple of times. The waitress arrives with the second or third Bahama

Mama for her. She places a chip on the waitress's tray, lights another cigarette. She counts the chips she has placed on the numbers. Thirteen. 13 is a good number, she should play it. She takes a chip from her stacks, places it smack center on 13. She is hot, she's in a winning groove, she is sipping a drink. Right on! 13! She's a winner. God bless the Bahamas.

"Hey, Robin," she calls, but Robin is glum-faced; she must be losing. The other players at the table, mostly elderly, are not exactly romantic candidates, but who cares? As long as her winning streak continues. Later, she'll find another table, with a younger, better-looking crowd, but for now she's fine, let her win some more.

Just take a look at her stacks! She has quite a few of them, neatly arranged in rows of ten. She counts them: twelve rows. A hundred and twenty bucks. She is seventy bucks ahead, plus the chips she has placed on the table for the next spin. She is drinking a Bahama Mama, her second or third. She shouldn't drink too much, not before she puts some food in her stomach. She is not even hungry—she hopes that Robin won't insist on taking a break and going for dinner.

She glances at Robin, then at the others. These old people, she reflects, seem as determined as she, they all want to win. Even if winning gets to be monotonous, anti-climactic, after a while. She has to thank Robin for introducing her to these games.

Right on, 17! She smiles, but, by now, is nearly indifferent, almost as if her winning were guaranteed. She's got two chips right on top. Seventy bucks coming her way.

"Let me have greens," she tells the croupier, and he slides toward her a stack of twenty chips with two green ones on top. The greens—twenty-five dollars each—she drops in her purse; now she will be playing with their money.

She draws on the cigarette, places her chips. All at once she realizes that Robin is not there—she stares at Robin's vacant seat. For a moment, she panics. Why did Robin leave without telling her?

Wait, calm down, she reasons with herself. Robin may have gone to the bathroom, she will be back shortly.

She scans the neighboring tables—perhaps Robin has gone there to change her luck. But Robin is not there.

She places her chips for the next spin, but her heart is no longer in the game, it feels heavy in her chest. Now she can't concentrate, her thoughts are fixed on Robin. Why does Robin have to ruin everything? Why can't she stick to their plan? Was Robin jealous because Maggie was winning?

What if, she contemplates a new possibility. What if Robin spotted Allen on the casino floor and went to join him? Fucking selfish Robin, why couldn't she say something before she left?

Here, she lost this round—27 comes out, a number she hates. Again she looks around her: No Robin, no Allen. Maybe that was the plan: To meet in the casino and drop her.

MAGGIE CASHES IN HER CHIPS AND stands in the aisle, uncertain about which way to turn. People push past her, she is in their way. Her stomach grumbles—she'd better eat something. She shouldn't have drunk on an empty stomach. How many did she have? Four, five drinks? Right this minute, how she'd love to go into one of the restaurants in the hotel, have a hearty meal, laugh with Robin, count her winnings. What is she supposed to do now? Wait here? Go upstairs? What if she left, and Robin came back, looking for her? Why doesn't Robin *think?*

Maggie swallows hard. She swallows pain, she swallows anger, she swallows the onslaught of bitter, self-pitying tears. She hates self-pity, but can never control or resist it; she always gives in. Feeling sorry for herself has become a sort of diversion.

A diversion from what? She is too tired to figure it out. She needs to pee. She'll go to the bathroom, then come back to the table to see if Robin has come for her.

In the bathroom, she gives the attendant a sad smile and goes into a stall. She peels off her pants, panties, and sits down. In the stall next to hers, a woman grunts with obvious relief, releasing a stream held in too long.

Maggie sighs. The poor attendant must listen all day to women peeing, wheezing, shitting, and then clean up after them. The mess women leave behind, the assorted stains and smudges on the white porcelain, the droplets of piss on the seat. It always amazes Maggie that women, purportedly neat and fussy at home, become so careless in public toilets, expecting other, "lesser" females to do their dirty work. She hates to admit this, but often she finds herself disliking women. When they think that no one is watching, they shed their polite pretense and are disrespectful. They think the world owes them. Granted, not all women—she herself is one—but women like Robin.

Coming out of the stall, she feels sad for herself, and for the attendant. She drops a quarter in the dish, nods to acknowledge the attendant's thanks. She walks back to the roulette tables; Robin is not there.

All right. She'll go upstairs. If Robin is there, fine. If Robin is not there, that's fine, too.

She inserts her key in the lock, opens the door. "Robin?" she calls. Nothing. Everything is just as they left it: the lights are on, as well as the TV.

Maggie drops her purse on the bed and gets the key to the robo-bar. She makes herself a drink of vodka and orange juice, unwraps a small Gouda cheese, breaks open a bag of potato chips. She'll have herself a nice little dinner, right here in the room. She is self-sufficient—this is one of her greatest gifts, her greatest achievements.

She spreads a large towel on Robin's bed to serve as table, pulls a few tissues from the box in the bathroom and folds them into a thick napkin. This will be her small revenge— let crumbs litter Robin's bed. And if Robin walks in while she eats, she'll apologize, saying she was too distraught to pay attention to such trivial details as whose bed it was.

She arranges the drink, the cheese, the potato chips on the towel and sits down to her meal. She begins to chew the food and surfs the channels, much like she does at home. As a matter of fact, she's actually enjoying herself. Perhaps, she muses, she doesn't need Robin. If Robin has chosen to forget about her, she can forget about Robin. She is ahead, she is winning, and that's what should really matter. Later, she'll go down again, try her luck at the blackjack tables. She'll play for as long as thirty dollars will last her. If she loses, it's all right, too; she'd still be playing with casino money.

How much is she ahead? She reaches for her purse and empties it out on the bed. One black chip, two green ones, and a red one—one hundred and fifty-five dollars. She started out with fifty: that means she is one hundred and five ahead.

She sips her drink and leans against the headboard,

smoking a cigarette and gazing at the twinkling lights out-side the glass doors. She could stay here forever. Live on the island, go swimming everyday. Train as a dealer and work in the casino. Forget about her puny life in New York. Forget textbook publishers, forget the tedious life of a copy editor who has to live on a meager budget. Budget—how she hates the word that has shaped her life for as long as she can remember and is so demeaning to a person of her sensibili-ties. She'll start a fresh, new life. Who knows, she might even meet Sean Connery. What's to stop her, except her fears, her insecurities?

She goes into the bathroom, applies fresh lipstick, smiles at the mirror and leaves the room—she is ready for more action. Walking down the hushed hallway she has a flash of the two of them, she and Robin, walking to the elevators, the excitement of the evening ahead of them. She still feels that excitement, but much less so. She prays that no one is there, waiting for the elevator; least of all a couple, or a couple of couples. How awkward she will feel, having to smile at them, having to act natural, friendly. In the elevator she prays that it doesn't stop at any of the floors. She feels especially vul-nerable when people can observe her from the back, at close range, noting every little defect.

Her prayers are answered, and she steps onto the shiny floor of the lobby, pulls back her shoulders and walks into the casino, her head held high. She'll find a nice, friendly table, have a couple of drinks, play her cards right and hope-fully win. She is usually lucky in cards. Unlucky in love? No. She is not willing, not yet, to allow such a negative conclu-sion.

Robin! she remembers with a smile. She hasn't thought about Robin for a while, which is good, very good. She won't allow Robin to put a damper on everything.

The casino is crowded. Everybody, it seems, has come out to gamble. She finds an empty seat at a five-dollar black-jack table, lays down two green chips, gets ten red ones; she'll play fifty, not thirty. What the hell, you live only once.

She places a chip in the white circle before her. She knows that for the first few hands, the other players, four men and two women, will be watching her, the newcomer, observing her every move. Judging from the fact that she's placed just one chip in the circle—the minimum—they'll surmise she's a careful gambler, or a novice; in their hearts they pray she knows what she is doing, hope she knows and plays by the rules.

She wants to reassure them: she knows the rules and mostly abides by them, she won't screw up their game. The dealer deals the cards, and she hopes for a blackjack—she's already got a picture card showing. She gets a two and silent-ly curses her bad luck. The dealer is showing a four. She's still got a chance, if they all play their cards right, and the dealer goes bust. She waves, No, at a third card, as do the others. The dealer flips over her hidden card. A picture. Good, pull another. The dealer pulls a third card. A picture! Relief. The players look up from the cards, smile, nod.

But the dealer doesn't smile, as she should when the table wins, it's the decent thing to do.

The man at the end seat says to the dealer, "You're very quiet tonight."

"I have a pain," the dealer says, and they all nod in sym-pathy.

"Where?" Maggie asks.

"My stomach."

"Let us win a couple of hands," says the man, "and you'll feel much better."

"Yeah!" says the dealer and they all laugh.

This is a good table, Maggie thinks, takes out her cigarettes. A cocktail waitress arrives, and Maggie orders a glass of water and a Screwdriver. She is going to win here, too, she can feel it, this must be her night. She watches the quick hands of the dealer, looks up at her name-tag: Lucia.

Maggie feels friendly. "Lucia," she calls before she has time to decide whether or not her question is witty and amusing. "Why do they call this game blackjack?"

Lucia looks at her, the others look at her. They smile, shrug; an awkward pause.

The man on her left rescues her. "In Europe," he says, "they call it twenty-one."

"I know," she says, smiles at him. He's a pleasant-looking man, well dressed, in his fifties; just friendly would be nice, nothing more. "Twenty-one makes sense, but blackjack?"

Her drink arrives and the man on her left lights her cigarette for her with his lighter. She is happy to have him at her side—he is so gentle, considerate. How she misses that, the feeling that someone is there to take care of her. She tosses her head, like Robin usually does, to get her hair away from her face. She inhales, exhales; she feels good. Only a short while ago, when looking for Robin, how miserable she felt! What a joke. Life is a joke. She should laugh more. Everyone should laugh more.

"Shuffle," Lucia says, and they sit and wait as she collects all the cards from the shoe and begins to shuffle them.

What a waste of time—Maggie stifles a sigh; she wishes Lucia were a little faster about this shuffling business.

"How many decks are we playing with?" asks the woman on Maggie's right.

Who cares? Maggie thinks. Just get the game going.

"Six," says Lucia.

What am I doing here? The thought suddenly sidles into

her mind. Me, Maggie, what am I doing here among all these gamblers? How pitiful I must look, just sitting here, waiting for cards.

She sits up. The least she can do is keep a straight posture, put an interested expression on her face. Look at all the old ladies playing the slots. They look as if they've been there forever, dropping coins in the machine, pulling the lever or hitting the spin button. Some of them are playing two or three machines at once. They seem to be in a hurry, oblivious to the small wins, waiting for the long, sharp wail of a jackpot win.

Finally, Lucia is done shuffling, and the players, revived, shift in their seats, ready for a fresh start.

"Be nice to us, we're all on welfare," the man at the end seat tells Lucia, and the table explodes.

"I do my best," Lucia says, allowing a smile. "But, you know, sometimes you eat the bear, sometimes the bear eats you."

"Tell me about it," says the man, and they all nod.

All right, Maggie thinks. Forget the bears, just deal me a good hand. Feeling lucky, she places two chips in the circle.

"Oh, there you are," she hears, and a radiant Robin, goddess-like, bends over and brushes her lips across Maggie's cheek.

Maggie stares at her—Robin has changed outfits. She is wearing a silky red dress and a pair of funky high heels. Robin's hair is loose, cascading down to her shoulders in soft waves. She looks like a woman from the movies whose trademark is danger. A woman like Sharon Stone.

"Where have you been?" Maggie finally says. "I looked all over for you."

"Shhh, Mag, don't get excited." Robin smiles benevolently. "Look," she says, pointing at the cards. "I've brought you luck."

Maggie looks at her cards: a shiny picture card and an ace—a blackjack!

"Where did you get this dress?" Maggie hears herself ask.

Robin laughs, but Maggie can hear the sharp edges in that laugh. "I'm going to have dinner, sweetie. I'll catch up with you later."

"Alone? You're having dinner alone?" Maggie asks as she anxiously watches the dealer; she wants to make sure she gets paid for the blackjack. Yet, she also wants Robin to wait for her. "I'll come with you," she says.

Robin whispers in her ear, "Don't cling, Maggie, you're making me nervous. It's my vacation, too, don't forget." Robin straightens up. "You stay right here like a good girl and win for us. Here, let's go partners." Robin drops two green chips on top of Maggie's stack. "I've been losing all night." Robin flashes a smile at the players around the table. How she charms them, Maggie thinks. She wants to collect her chips and get up from the table, but Robin is already walking away.

"Wait," Maggie calls after her, but Robin only waves and then is gone.

"She'll be back," says the pleasant-looking man at her side.

"I know," Maggie says, distractedly. Who is Robin having dinner with? Allen? Why has she changed outfits?

She mustn't look dejected, she tells herself. The players at the table mustn't get the impression she is dependent on Robin.

"She's my younger sister," she tells the table, gives a little smile. "I feel responsible, she may lose her head."

"I wish I had a sister like that to look after," says the man at the end seat, and they all laugh. At first Maggie worries it was meant as a putdown; then she joins in the laughter.

"Money is not a problem," she continues. "It is just that she...." Maggie doesn't complete the sentence, but leaves it hanging. As she was speaking she realized she was about to say that Robin is loose, then thought better of it. The players glance up at her, then look down at their cards.

"When did you get here?" asks the pleasant-looking man.

"Today," she says. "It's my first time here."

"Oh," says the man, "you're going to like it. Me and my wife, we come here regularly. At least four or five times a year."

"Really?" she says, not surprised to hear that he is married, he looks like the married type. She is still thinking about Robin. How glamorous she looked in her red dress, her flowing hair. Even if she owned such a dress, she'd never have the nerve to wear it. Now again she feels deflated, wishing that Robin had never come to the table.

THE NEXT MORNING, SHE WAKES UP WITH a headache. She squints against the light; last night, she forgot to draw the curtains, and the hot, bright sun is directly on her. She turns onto her side, notices Robin's empty, smooth bed. So, Robin hasn't come back. Last night, she remembers, she locked the door, but did not bolt it with the chain, in case Robin....

But Robin, it is obvious, spent the night in someone

else's bed. This is the last time she goes anywhere with Robin. Unless Robin comes up with a very good excuse. But even if she does, even if she says she wanted to sleep with Allen, still, the least she should have done was to call and leave a message.

Fuck Robin. Maggie tosses the covers and gets out of bed, swallows a couple of aspirins. She goes under the shower, then remembers she'll be swimming soon, there's no point in taking a shower. She pulls a towel from the rack and dries herself, spreads toothpaste across her brush. As she looks at herself in the mirror, at her hand moving briskly up and down her white teeth, her healthy, pink gums, the night before comes back in a flash. She didn't stay long at the blackjack table. She cashed in her chips and went to look for Robin in the restaurants of the hotel. Feeling like a shadow, she walked in and out of the restaurants, nervously, desperately, straining her eyes in the dimly lit rooms, wishing to spot the red dress. Finally, giving up, she went back to the casino and played some more. At one point, she thought she glimpsed Robin across the casino floor. She hurried in that direction, but lost her in the crowd. She remained downstairs until four in the morning, ending up at a roulette table with a few stray, male gamblers, all definitely losers. From the vacant expression on their faces, she gathered they were hoping, at the very last moments before closing time, to regain some of their losses. What am I doing? she asked herself with mounting self-hate, but couldn't, wouldn't, pull herself away. Doggedly, she stayed at the table until the pit boss called it a night. She collected her remaining chips and walked to the elevator, trying to maintain a dignified, erect posture, praying that no one was watching or following her.

She is such a phony, such a frightened, little phony. She doesn't like to think it, but it's true. Did she win or lose last

night? She can't remember. She rinses out her mouth, goes
back into the room and empties out her purse. Thank God,
she still has some money left, she is still seventy dollars
ahead. Actually, only twenty, counting the fifty dollars Robin
gave her. But fuck Robin. She'll tell her she's lost it all.

Seventy dollars. All right, not bad, not as bad as she
feared. This might yet turn out to be a great vacation. She has
a luxurious, double room all to herself—a tropical kingdom.
Now she won't mind it at all if Robin moves in with Allen, or
whomever she spent the night with. Let her remain where
she is. Let Robin fuck her brains out; she'd hear all the sor-
did details on the plane back.

The plane back. She doesn't want to think about the
plane back.

She puts on a long T-shirt over her bathing suit, drops
Vanity Fair into her shoulder bag and glances at the room
one last time before shutting the door. She walks to the elevators, feeling worldly, on top of things. No more skimping!
She'll have a full breakfast downstairs and charge it to the
room. While eating, she'll leisurely read her magazine, or
just look around, observing the others.

What if she meets Robin and Allen? Nothing. She'll be
polite, insist on having her breakfast alone; she doesn't want
to be bothered. She'll have eggs over-easy, bacon, fries. Rye
toast and jam. Coffee. A glass of cold water. She won't mind
eating alone, she'll savor it. Every drop. Every morsel. She'll
project an aloof, worldly demeanor. She doesn't need Robin.
All she need do is mentally adjust to the new situation.

Her bill comes to twelve dollars. An expensive breakfast,
but so what? She can afford it, she is on vacation. She looks
over the large elegant room, so airy, sunny, with white table-
cloths and stiff napkins. It's pretty crowded with breakfast
diners—she's the only one eating alone. But she doesn't mind

it. In fact, eating alone makes her special. And there's no sign of Robin, of Allen. They're probably having breakfast in bed. Before and after sex.

A twinge of jealousy tugs at her heart. Robin is having a good time, while she....Well, she, too, is having a good time. Once she gets Robin out of her thoughts she'll have an even better time.

Feeling a bit subdued, she goes down to the beach and pulls a chaise longue under an umbrella. Is she happy? No, not right this minute. But she is doing OK. She is calm, relaxed, she is doing fine on her own. Later, she'll go to the casino—that's where she can truly let go of everything and have a good time.

From under the umbrella, she avidly follows the movements of an older couple she has noticed at breakfast. A young girl is with them—their granddaughter, she surmises. Grandpa takes pictures of wife and child as they stand and smile in the water. He then puts away the camera and joins them. She hears them laugh, and it comforts her. It is good, she reflects, to see people enjoy themselves; she would have liked to join in their happiness. Days come and go and, in the end, what is left? At times, how empty and futile everything seems: money, ambition, even love.

Grandpa comes out of the water and pulls his chair to the shade. Lying down, his hands behind his head, how comfortable he seems, and content. Grandma comes out of the water, and Maggie watches him watch his wife approach. What does he see? she wonders. Her wrinkled, jelly-like thighs? The woman whose hands cooked his meals for many years? Does he feel compassion for her aging flesh, or does he resent her aging for it reminds him of his own?

She sighs—time to go in for a swim. How soothing the water is, how comforting. This is where unpleasant thoughts evaporate. She flips over, shuts her eyes and floats on her back. She is all alone, suspended between sky and water. Tears push into her eyes, but she tells herself she mustn't cry. She must fight her gloomy mood, she is on vacation. It's costing her a lot, more than she can afford, to be here. She'd better pull herself together and make the most of this long overdue vacation. Robin owes her nothing, and, like Robin said last night, it's her vacation, too: she must remember not to forget that and let Robin have her space.

Still floating on her back, Maggie imagines how her body, like a piece of driftwood, is gently maneuvered by the current. What keeps her afloat? Determination. She could relax her spine, let herself sink and drop to the bottom. She could, but she won't. She is alive, far away from her life in a city she loves, but also hates. Her good friend Robin is a fitting representative of that city: hard, cruel, seductive. Dangerous? Yes, the city is dangerous. The ocean could be dangerous too; she's been floating on her back for quite a while. Who knows how far she's drifted. Should she turn over and look? No, not yet, she likes flirting with danger; Robin doesn't know this about her. She sees Robin in her red dress and funky high heels, her long hair flowing down her shoulders like rays of light. Let Robin have a good time. Then she'll tell Maggie all about it.

Maggie turns over. All at once it hits her: Robin might be in danger. Too quickly, too readily, she assumed that Robin had abandoned her. Just the opposite might be the case. And if Robin is in danger, she is in danger, too: whoever is holding Robin, has the key to their room. It seems a bit fantastic that Robin is being held against her will, and yet it's possible. They're in a foreign country, with rules and codes all its own.

Frantically, she swims back, panic constricting her breath. It feels as though she is swimming in place, making no progress. Panting, she reaches the shore, gathers her things and hurries up the stairs, across the pool area. She enters the lobby and stands there a moment, adjusting to the cool air, the dim light, the noise of a busy, international hotel. So many people coming and going, talking. She is just one, feeling so alone among them. They don't know her situation, and even if they did, they wouldn't really care. Is she over-reacting? Why does she see danger everywhere? And yet, better safe than sorry: she must report that Robin is missing. At least, as far as she knows, Robin is missing. But who can she talk to, and what will she say? That her girlfriend has disappeared the night before? Why didn't she alert them sooner? Because, she'll say. I thought my friend met someone. Met someone? Should she mention Allen? Allen who? She doesn't even know his last name. She'd better not mention him, or they'll assume the obvious. She doesn't want them to assume the obvious; she wants them to look for Robin.

IT IS FREEZING IN THE LOBBY. SHIVERING, she goes over to the information desk and asks to speak to security.

"Security?" The man eyes her with a stony face. "What seems to be the problem?"

Seems to be? Is he doubting her?

"My girlfriend disappeared," she says, listening to herself as the incongruous words leave her mouth. Should she have phrased it differently? "Disappeared" does sound overly dramatic.

"Are you a guest in the hotel?" he asks as if he hadn't heard what she said.

"Of course I am," she blurts. What else would she be doing here, speaking to him? How dense he is, or pretends to be. She won't let him get to her.

She hugs herself. "I'm freezing," she adds, just so that he knows she intends to ignore his self-important attitude.

But it is hard for her to ignore his attitude. She has to look at him, tell him her story. She hates the way he looks at her, his face a dark, impassive mask, his eyes cold and unblinking. She wishes she'd gone upstairs and changed before speaking to this person. Already he is suspicious, probably concluding she's just another flaky American tourist. She mustn't, *mustn't* burst into tears.

"What do you mean, disappeared?" he asks, indifferent, unmoved, his big, fat lips pinkish on the inside. She is not a racist, she doesn't think, but right this minute she hates this man, and this man happens to be black, an arrogant native of this island. He should be more agreeable to tourists, not to say, hospitable. He makes his living off her.

"Just that, disappeared," she says, her voice betraying her irritation. And since she's already let her indignation show, she is openly belligerent. "Do I need to raise my voice for you to understand? She disappeared, goddamit. I want you to find her."

She sees a flicker of anger cross his dark features, and is glad for it.

Without a word, he moves away from her and picks up the telephone.

Thank God, she thinks, turns her back on him and leans against the counter. Let him do his job. Let them all do their jobs and find Robin. Tears sting in her nostrils; she's all alone, having to contend with unfriendly natives.

She hears him whisper into the telephone. Is she behaving irrationally? Hysterically? What else can she do? She must assume that Robin is in trouble.

Unless—a doubt creeps into her mind. What if Robin is up in the room? What if she has spent the night and now is back? She can just hear Robin yelling at her, "I can't go fuck someone without you calling the police?"

But it's too late to retract her story. A tall man in uniform approaches her and she straightens up, readying herself. He goes around the counter, and she turns to face the two of them. The information clerk stands up, and now it's two dark giants looking down on her. She tells them her room number, her name, the last time she saw Robin. She gets caught up in the urgency of her story, tears swell in her eyes. "You must find her," she tells the security man. "It's unlike her to disappear like that." Tears are streaming down her cheeks. "I'm going out of my mind with worry. I'm all alone here and I'm scared."

"No need to cry," says the security man, handing her a tissue.

"I know," she says, "but I can't help myself." She blows her nose. They must believe her. They must listen and take her seriously.

The security man murmurs something to the clerk, then turns to her. "Let's go up to the room," he says.

Up to the room? She hesitates. What for? What is she getting herself into?

But she has no choice, she must follow him. They walk the length of the lobby, and she tries to keep pace with him. His walkie-talkie, clipped onto his belt, emits the usual sounds of static. People glance their way as if they sense that something is not right. She wonders if she is safe going upstairs with this man.

"Why are we going upstairs?" she asks.

He glances at her, his expression blank and detached. "I want to take a look around."

Of course she is safe, he's from security, he won't risk his job. And he is not bad-looking, he is actually handsome. A perfectly shaped skull, round and noble. Good shoulders, a muscular figure.

"We're quite a sight," she tries to joke as they wait for the elevator. He looks at her and shrugs. No sense of humor, she concludes. Why bother trying to be friendly?

Upstairs, she unlocks the door and is relieved to see that Robin is not there. The maid hasn't been to the room yet, so he can see for himself that only one bed was slept in. He steps inside, walks to the veranda and back, then asks to see Robin's luggage. What for? she wonders, but goes to the closet and opens it. "It's all here." She points at Robin's things. "See? I didn't make her up."

"I didn't say you did."

She pouts. "What now?"

He pulls the walkie-talkie off his belt and places it on the table. He relaxes his stance. "Did you two have a fight?" he asks.

She looks at the walkie-talkie. Why did he take it off? It crosses her mind she'd better put on some clothes and not stand there in her T-shirt, stained at the breasts by her wet bathing suit.

"No," she says. "Of course not. At any rate, she wouldn't just leave. I mean, where could she go?"

The man nods, thoughtfully. He seems more sympathetic. He seems to believe her.

"Yesterday," she continues, "Robin met a man on the beach. His name is Allen, or that's what he told us. He's a guest at the hotel, and he, too, arrived yesterday."

"Maybe she's with him." The man smiles in that obvious way she knew people would if she mentioned Allen. "Or, are you suggesting she was kidnapped?"

She shrugs. It does seem absurd that Robin would let herself be kidnapped from a crowded casino. "I don't know. She's gone, that's all I know. Maybe she wasn't kidnapped. Maybe she's having a great time somewhere. But I had to tell you. Someone."

"You did the right thing," the man says, and she feels enormously relieved. "We see it all the time, two women, travelling alone...."

She looks at him. What is he suggesting? "Yes?" she says, waiting for more.

He throws his palms up in the air, a gesture that reminds her of her father. "Sometimes there's a conflict. One wants to do one thing, the other, something else." He smiles, reassuringly. "I suggest in the meantime that you go on with your vacation. It's your vacation, too, isn't it?"

"Well, yes." She pretends to be considering this new revelation. "But she's my friend, and I worry."

"Of course she's your friend," he says, "and I'm confident she'll turn up. If you had a picture, though, it would help."

"A picture?"

"A photograph. Of your friend. So we'd have a better idea who we're looking for."

A photograph. Of course. "Wait," she says, goes into the closet and pulls out Robin's backpack and shakes its contents out on the bedspread. "She must have her driver's license, or some other picture I.D."

She feels a bit funny, going through Robin's things, but she's enduring all this trouble, and wasting precious vacation time, for Robin's sake.

No driver's license, no picture I.D., just a packet of tissues, a couple of rubber bands, a pocket calendar, an empty wallet. She senses the man standing over her, and is again aware of her exposed legs, the open cut of her T-shirt.

All at once, she feels defeated, it is all so pointless. She wants him to leave, she wants to be left alone.

She stands up. "Nothing," she says.

"Could you describe her for me?"

"Describe her?" Yes, she could. She could describe Robin.

"She's on the plump side," she begins, "like sort of my height, but a little heavier." She looks at him—he seems to be interested, even encouraging. "She has beautiful hair, shoulder length, sort of honey-reddish, Irish-reddish...." She pauses. What does he know from Irish-reddish? "Her skin is creamy, very smooth, and her eyes are sort of hazel. She is very attractive, very sweet-looking." As she talks, it occurs to her that she is describing Robin as if Robin were for sale.

"Right," he says, picking up his walkie-talkie and moving to the door. "Let me know if she turns up."

She follows behind, small against his tall frame. "That's it? I mean, do you have a card? So I could call you?"

"Good thinking," he says, fishing a card out of his breast pocket. "Enjoy the rest of your vacation."

"I will," she says wearily and shuts the door.

Now what? she thinks as she turns to face the empty room. It's almost noon. It's too hot to be outdoors. She'll take a shower. She'll make herself a drink. Relax. She'll go down to the casino for a while, then have a late lunch-early dinner. Perhaps the guy—what's his name? She looks at the card: Wynston Foster. Perhaps Wynston was right. Robin was somewhere, having fun, making the most of her vacation. She should do the same, that's why she spent the money to come here, all the way to Paradise Island.

She draws the curtains, lies down on the bed and shuts her eyes. She feels a little tired. She'll rest a while, and when the maid arrives to clean the room, she'll go down to the casino and gamble for an hour or so. Then, in the late afternoon, she may go back to the beach and swim some more. Or, maybe she won't. Like Robin says, she doesn't have to plan everything in advance. If only Robin came back, how relieved she would be.

And yet, she is not sure she is not liking this better. All alone in the room. At this hour. With the curtains drawn. A hushed calm, homey and quiet. Now time stands still. It's almost as if it doesn't exist. She floats, drifts, as she does in the water.

How strange people are, unpredictable. Why would Robin invite her to come along, and then drop her? Because Robin is a screwed-up bitch. She dragged Maggie along as a safety measure, just in case. How come Robin instantly finds herself a man, whereas she doesn't? Without meaning to, she scares men off.

A knock on the door startles her. She sits up, prepares to answer it, but hears a key inserted in the lock. Robin! she thinks, and her heart begins to beat faster. Immediately, she lies down and shuts her eyes. Why does her heart flutter so? How ridiculous she is, pretending to be asleep.

"Oh, sorry, Miss," she hears and opens her eyes. The maid. A middle-aged woman and her vacuum cleaner.

"Sorry, Miss, I'll come back later."

The subservient tone annoys her. The sudden appearance of the maid annoys her. Sophia it says on her name tag. Shortish, maternal, not black exactly, maybe brown. Hispanic?

"No," she mutters, "it's all right. I wish, though, you came earlier."

"I'm very sorry, Miss."

"I have to take a shower, but you can clean the room."

"Thank you, Miss."

She goes into the bathroom, peels off her bathing suit, lets it drop to the floor. Let the maid clean after her. After all, she is a maid, and it is her job. It's time she demanded to be catered to. The more ruthless one is, the more service one gets. That's the paramount lesson she's learned from Robin. It's time she paid attention to her own feelings, instead of worrying about the feelings of others.

She comes out of the shower, dries herself, then drops the towel to the floor. Naked, she goes back into the room and begins to comb her hair. There's no reason for her to be timid about her nakedness around the maid. Normally, one is oblivious of the help. Let the maid gorge her eyes on the white, privileged body of her young mistress.

Through the mirror, as she gets dressed, Maggie watches the maid make the bed. Sophia bends and, with strong, brown arms, pulls the sheet tight across. Maggie can see the strain in the woman's back, in her face, and for a split second she regrets her thoughts, her behavior.

"Thank you, Sophia," she says and stands there a moment, undecided. She wants to say more, she wants to apologize, but the maid, she fears, won't understand what she is apologizing for.

Sophia, holding a pillow in her hands, looks at her and smiles, waiting.

"I'm leaving now, Sophia," Maggie says in a soft, child-like voice.

"Good, Miss. Have a nice time."

IN THE CASINO, SHE WALKS AROUND AIMLESSLY, imagining how she bumps into Robin and acts as if nothing has happened, not saying a word about Robin disappearing on her, and not mentioning Wynston, the security guy. She also entertains another scenario, where Robin comes up to the room, sobbing, her face bruised, her beautiful red dress torn at the shoulder. It turns out that the guy she was with was a real psychopath, he tied her up and beat her....

Maggie looks at her watch. It's nine o'clock in the evening. She had soup for dinner at one of the snack bars, played blackjack for a while where she won and lost and won and lost and finally left the table more or less even. It is too early to go to sleep, but she could go upstairs and read. She doesn't feel like gambling, is afraid she'll give away her winnings. Once in a while, she stops at a table and observes the players, the dealers. They're an interesting bunch, she reflects. Both dealers and players. The players don't look too happy as they sit there at the table, placing their bets. Some look downright miserable, and she feels sorry for them. It's hard to tell what the dealers think; she watches them, tries to penetrate the masks they wear.

A commotion erupts at one of the tables, and she hurries in that direction. Two women are going at it, flinging themselves at one another, kicking and scratching, drawing blood. Maggie watches them, mesmerized. Just like men, she marvels, not giving a damn about pain or physical injury. They're both young and sort of wild-looking in their miniskirts, leather boots, and unruly long hair. Why doesn't someone do something, Maggie thinks, but presently, as if from nowhere, security people descend on the scene and pull the women apart and away. The women continue to scream and kick, hurling curse words at one another, and at the security men. People look at each other and smile, shrug, then continue to play. "I tell you," a tall big man says, shaking his head.

The excitement over, Maggie continues on. Again, she looks at her watch: nine-thirty. She is tired of walking. She'll go upstairs and read for a while. She doesn't have to gamble every night, she'll be smart, hold on to her gains. Tomorrow is another day. Vacation means fun, but also rest, and she could use some; she didn't sleep much the night before, so tonight she'll catch up. And she likes her state of mind, so calm and reasonable, so self-possessed.

Upstairs, she immediately notices that the backpack is not on the bed, and yet, she distinctly remembers leaving it there. The maid wouldn't have touched it, so it must be Robin. So she did come back, the slut, and left again. Living the high life, big time. Maggie opens the closet; indeed, the backpack is there, and so is the red dress. She sniffs it—a faint trace of sweat and Robin's sweet perfume. She pulls the dress off the hanger, then, hurriedly, takes off her clothes and tries it on.

Not a bad fit, if a bit loose around the waist and tummy—she turns in front of the mirror this way and that, approving of what she sees: the dress beautifully highlights her features, calls attention to her face, her exposed chest. So this is what she must do. The right outfit makes things happen. But fucking Robin told her to pack light, and she did. Not that she has something in her wardrobe that even remotely resembles this dress. She does have a nice enough black dress, high heels, but she left them at home. She could borrow a dress from Robin, or confiscate this one, but she'd need high heels, and Robin wears a gigantic eight-and-a-half shoe, whereas Maggie's foot is a dainty elegant six. The one thing Robin often says she is envious of, are Maggie's small feet and perfect toes.

Looking at herself in the mirror, Maggie pulls off the dress and lets it drop to the floor. Actually, the dress stinks with Robin's odor, with the scent of her nauseating perfume. Even if she did have the right shoes, she wouldn't wear it. The notion of Robin's sweat touching her skin is too revolting, sickening in fact. She kicks the dress under the commode.

S HE HEARS THEM WHISPER, LIKE TWO conspirators, but keeps her eyes shut, pretending to be asleep. How considerate they are, Robin and some guy, sneaking in quietly, whispering, turning on the light in the bathroom. Do they mean to fuck with her in the room, or did they just come in to pick something up? The room is half in darkness, she can open her eyes without them noticing. She sees their silhouettes, getting stuff out of the closet. A new outfit for Robin? What time is it? Must be past midnight. She stayed awake till eleven and then switched off the light and fell asleep. They're unzipping Robin's bags and suit bag. Are they looking for the red dress? If they find it under the commode, she'll say she has no idea how it got there. They're getting stuff out of drawers. Is Robin packing? Yes, she is!

Maggie switches on the lamp light and sits up. "What's going on?" she asks.

"Oh, you're awake, sweetie." Robin comes toward her.

"I wasn't before. Now I am." Maggie rubs her eyes.

"I'm sorry we woke you. Something came up and I had

to get my stuff."

"What do you mean?"

"I want you to meet Ben," Robin says, and Ben approaches the bed. Ben my man, Maggie singsongs contemptuously in her head.

"Ben, this is my good friend, Maggie."

"I've heard so much about you." Ben shakes her hand. He's so ugly, she thinks, so old. For one thing, whatever blond hair he has left on his head looks dry and stringy. His lips are too thick, especially the bottom one which sort of droops toward his chin. She can hardly believe that Robin would go for someone like him.

"Sorry we disturbed you," Ben continues. "But, like Robin said...." He turns to Robin. "Why don't I take the bags downstairs and wait for you?"

"Good idea," Robin says. "Just take the bags, I'll manage the suit bag."

Just like a married couple—Maggie feels disgust rise in her again. "I'm all confused," she says once Ben is out the door.

"What about, sweetie?" Robin sits down on the bed.

"Why is he taking your bags?"

"We're going sailing."

"At this hour?"

"Why not?" Robin giggles. "We'll be back in a couple of days."

"In a couple of days?!"

"Yes, sweetie."

"No, you won't."

"Mag, please, have I ever lied to you?"

"Then why are you taking all your stuff?"

"Because," Robin explains forbearingly. "I don't know what I might need."

"Whatever happened to Allen?"

Robin waves her hand. "Gone with the wind."

"So, you're leaving me." Maggie hangs her head.

"I'm not leaving you, I'm going sailing. It's my vacation, remember?"

"Why can't I come with you?"

"Because." Robin is exasperated. "I didn't plan it, you know. I met him last night, and I like him a lot, and I want to spend some time with him. I can't spring a friend on him. It's a small yacht and he wants to be alone with me."

"You mean, he sailed all the way to the Bahamas alone? These guys, as far as I know, usually sail with friends."

"Maybe, I don't know, Maggie, please don't pester me."

She can see through Robin's lies. "All I'm trying to say is that he looks suspicious to me."

Robin laughs gaily. "Don't be ridiculous, he's a friend of friends, you needn't worry."

"I'm not worried. It's just that he looks so old."

"Well." Robin turns cold. "I like them old." She stands up and goes to her bed and picks up the suit bag. "By the way, I can't find my red dress."

Maggie shrugs. "I didn't see it."

Robin looks around her. "I wonder where it can be. I'm sure I hung it in the closet."

"Don't look at me, I have no idea."

"Hmmm." Robin thinks. "Was someone else in the room?"

"How should I know? You don't think I sit up here all day, keeping watch?"

"Relax, Maggie, it doesn't matter."

"Maybe the maid took it." Maggie gets out of bed. She's only in her panties, but, so what? "Actually, now that I think of it." She looks at Robin and smiles slyly. "I did have someone come up to the room, but why would he take your dress, I can't imagine. Unless"—Maggie strikes a pensive pose. "Unless he thought it was mine and took it as a souvenir?"

"You had someone up here?"

"Well, yes, why not?" Maggie giggles. "Fuck our brains out, remember?"

Robin looks at her. "You're acting very strange, Mag. I don't like it."

"Don't you worry your little head. Just go out there and have fun with Ben your man."

"Thank you," Robin says. "I will."

At the door, Robin stops. "Aren't you going to kiss me goodbye?"

"Of course." Maggie goes up to Robin and kisses her on the cheek. All at once, Robin seems small, defenseless.

"I'll see you in a couple of days," Robin says.

"Sure. I'll be here."

"If my dress turns up...."

"Don't worry, I'll keep it for you."

She shuts the door and bolts it with the chain—now, even if they want to, they can't come in. She retrieves the dress from under the commode and shakes it out. What is she going to do with it? She'll give it to Sophia, that's what she'll do. The maid is sure to have a daughter, or a niece, who could put it to good use. Robin has too many clothes as it is. And she's going on a yacht with a rich old man. He can afford to buy her another red dress, or a dozen red dresses. He'll finance all her whims, he'll pay for her chin-lifts, tummy-tucks, liposuctions. For all her brave talk about careers, about "making it," Robin will become what she's always wanted to be: a highly paid slut.

SHE IS ON A ROLL, PLAYING CARIBBEAN POKER. The first night, when she played blackjack, the pleasant-looking guy told her about the game. He said his wife loved Caribbean Poker, was a pro at it, but that Maggie shouldn't even go near it. You can lose a lot, and *fast*—he snapped his fingers.

But here she is, at the table, her head spinning, her heart racing. She was drawn to the table, like a magnet, pulled a chair and sat down. And she is ahead, she is winning, she is invincible. If the guy's wife can play it, she can, too. Indeed, it's costing her sixteen bucks a pop to be in the game—the man was right: you can lose a lot—but she is winning. And how quickly she took to the game, picked up the rules. She is drinking a Bahama Mama, is ready for another; she loves the pink, thick drink. Here's the cocktail waitress in her starched uniform—a black skirt, a white shirt—unlike the absurd, tits-and-ass costume they make them wear in Atlantic City. They respect their women here, which is a good thing.

She orders another Bahama Mama and lights a cigarette. The people at the table are elderly, Florida-types; she is the youngest. She likes being the youngest, especially when they adopt a parental attitude toward her. The blond woman on her left, apologizing, asks for a cigarette. Sure, Maggie says expansively and hands the woman the full pack. She likes the camaraderie at the table; they are all seasoned gamblers, and she is one of them.

She drops a dollar chip in the slot allotted to her. This extra dollar will land the jackpot in her lap: all she need do is be dealt a royal straight flush and win five hundred grand. That's half a million. Not bad for a night's work. How her life will change. She'll be generous, will give a couple of thousand to each player, and, naturally, to the dealer.

She can see it coming, the big win, and mutely rehearses what she'll say, how she'll announce her good fortune once the cards are firmly in her hand: a nice, once-in-a-lifetime royal straight flush staring her in the face. A wonderful sort of calm will settle in her heart, for she'll never have to worry about money again. She can't even imagine such a fortunate, care-free existence, but she'll take to it, oh yes, she will. When the providential cards are dealt to her, she'll keep her cool, raise her voice just a notch and tell the dealer: "All right! You don't have to qualify, but it will be nice if you do. I hit the jackpot, yes, the jackpot."

Oh, God, yes. It can happen, why not, she deserves a break. Let Robin eat her heart out. She can see Robin's face turn green when she tells her about winning the jackpot. She can see Robin getting seasick on the yacht.

The blonde hands her back the pack of cigarettes and tells her she came in on a cruise from Florida. Maggie nods. She's never gone on a cruise. It now occurs to her that since she's arrived, she hasn't left the hotel. She has yet to go touring, visit the pink hotel across the water. Never mind. What's so special about a pink hotel?

She is dealt a flush—good! Five beautifully uniform, stark spades. She'll get fifty dollars from the jackpot, and if the dealer qualifies—with a king and ace or better—she'll get another sixty.

The jackpot. The queenpot. This thought, in a flash, brings back a dream she had last night, and she sees again the four, shiny queens that were dealt to her. At this table, four queens could mean a few thousand. Quite a few thousand.

The dealer doesn't qualify, but she gets her fifty dollars from the jackpot. The other players congratulate her: they like to see a good hand. A good hand gives them all hope; they may get one, too. It is all in the cards, all in the cards.

She collects her winnings, tips the dealer. How she hates players who don't tip the dealer after a win.

"Why," she asks the table, "don't they call it the queen-pot?"

Everyone smiles, shrugs. The bald man, who smokes a fat cigar and plays his black, one-hundred-dollar chips as if they were dimes, says, "You're absolutely right, young lady. They should call it the queenpot."

"Women already have the pot," the blond Floridian says. "The kitchen pot."

"That's a good one." Everybody laughs, even the dealer. Maggie laughs, too. She admires the wide, generous decollete of the blonde. The woman must be in her sixties, yet her skin is still smooth, slightly tan. Indeed, Maggie thinks, she was lucky to find just the right table. She's among friends.

Friends? Well, not exactly. As soon as she leaves, she'll never see these people again, but right now they're exactly what she needs.

The blonde coughs—the deep, resounding cough of a veteran smoker, and Maggie reflects that she, too, will end up sounding like this if she doesn't quit. But she will quit—she has time on her side, she is still young—even if she secretly covets the reckless decadence a smoking life implies. If only she had it in her to become more free and less cautious.

Again, Robin crosses her mind—but this time as a shadow, a name, not as a person. Perhaps she should get something to eat. She feels a bit dizzy. She could go for a sandwich, a nice tuna-fish sandwich, but she doesn't want to leave the table. She'd better not think about food. She can order another drink, smoke another cigarette.

But she needs to go to the bathroom. "I'll be right back," she tells the dealer, and stands up. Stoutly she marches toward the sign "Women," her head a bit heavy, wobbly, on her neck, her eyes drooping. Her legs, too, feel wooden, and she's aware of each step as if walking were unnatural to the human form.

She forgot her watch upstairs—what time is it? Impossible to tell whether it's night or day. The world outside could blow to pieces and they'd never know it, not in the casino. She must remember how to find her way back. She is walking straight, then right, and reaches the bathroom. When she comes out, she'll have to turn left, then walk straight until she finds the table. Very simple.

She goes into a stall and locks the door, pulls down her pants and lands on the seat. God, she is heavy, she feels heavy. She leans forward and shuts her eyes. She could go upstairs and take a short nap. Bad idea. If she falls asleep, she'll sleep till morning, miss a whole night's action.

She'll drink water. No more of those sexy Bahama Mamas, or Screwdrivers. She'll switch to beer. Beer is grain, it will fill her up. The carbonated bubbles will shoot straight to her brain, will sober her up.

She comes out of the stall, slowly walks toward the mirror. She hears the door open and turns to look. A man in a dark print shirt appears in the doorway, and for a terrifying moment they stare at each other, her heart beating in her throat. Where is the attendant? How come she is all alone? She notes the man's dark eyes, his curly hair, and is paralyzed, thinking he is going to come after her, rob or rape her. If he does, she'll remember his features, they're etched on her brain. But just as soon, the man is gone, and the door slams shut, and she tells herself it's nothing, nothing, just a guy who's made an honest mistake. She mustn't freak out so easily, yet she's a woman alone, she must be on guard.

A bit shaken, she leans over the sink, splashes water on her face, rinses her mouth. She looks a bit tired, but still presentable. Robin would have chided her if Robin were there. Robin would have dragged her from the table and put some food in her stomach. She needs Robin. Fucking Robin. She remembers how she glorified Robin in her description, so that Wynston would be diligent in his search. Robin's long hair, her silky lashes, her silky eyebrows that have never been plucked. You want to lick her face, she could have said, it's that smooth.

Here, she's washed her face and applied fresh lipstick, which helps a lot. Her eyes still have a glassy look, but her skin radiates a healthy, reddish glow from the sun. This type of climate is good for her skin. Her skin likes the sun, the salty moisture in the air.

She comes out of the bathroom, stands a moment, undecided. Then she recalls. She turns left, then walks straight ahead. It must be night time. The casino is crowded, noisy, and live music is spilling from one of the bars. Everybody is out to have a good time. She, too, is having a good time, a great time. When did she start playing? Around two in the afternoon, when she came back from the beach.

She approaches the table, her vacant seat. As she pulls her chair, the dealer says, "Sorry, Miss, this seat is taken."

"I know." She smiles. "It's mine."

She looks down at the table. Her chips are gone! She left them right there, and now they're gone! She looks up. The people around the table look at her strangely—they look unfriendly, even hostile. They're all strangers.

"You must be mistaken," says the dealer, helpfully. "Try the next table."

She feels herself blush; they must think she's a fluke, a

drunken fluke. She turns from them, walks over to the next table. There they are, her friends. The blonde, the man with the cigar. She is so relieved. And her chips are there, her blessed chips. It seems as though she's been gone forever.

She pulls her chair and sits down. Someone must have left, for a new player—a young guy—is seated to her right.

She places her bet—she'll be included in the next hand. She looks around for the cocktail waitress. Come on, come on, be here already. I want my beer, my glass of water. She revels in her wants, in her impetuousness.

She lights a cigarette, exhales the smoke to the mirrored ceiling. Someone up there is always watching, monitoring the cameras. She wonders if they pay special attention to her, if she stands out. She'd love to be allowed up there, just for the sense of privilege. Where's that cocktail waitress?

"Excuse me," she asks the new guy on her right. "Do you have the time?"

"Sure." The guy looks at his watch. She looks, too, waiting. She tries to concentrate. "Ten-thirty," he says.

Ten-thirty?!

"Impossible," she says.

The guy laughs. "Time flies when you're having fun." He shows her his watch. It's not one of those bulky ones young macho guys usually wear; it's sort of elegant. She focuses her gaze on the digits. Indeed, it's ten-thirty.

"I hope," he says, "it's not serious."

"Serious?"

"Whatever it is you had to do."

"No." She looks at him. She sort of likes him. He seems gentle, polite, considerate. "I was going to make a phone call," she says, just so that he knows she is not alone, "but it doesn't matter."

The man with the cigar wins big, and they all cheer and

applaud. He has a straight and the dealer qualifies. For the man with the cigar who is a high roller and plays only with black chips, it's a thousand-dollar hand. The waitress arrives and Maggie orders a beer, a glass of water.

"I had a flush before you joined us," Maggie tells the guy. "The dealer didn't qualify, but I had a dollar in the slot."

"Good for you," the guy says. "That's why we sit here. You must go for the jackpot."

"Oh, do I ever." She laughs.

The waitress places her beer before her and thankfully she tips her, drinks the beer. Ah, it's so good. She'd better not gulp it down, just in case the guy is watching. Like her, he plays with five-dollar chips, bets the minimum; he is not a high roller.

"Where are you from?" she asks. It's a direct question, but it's all right—she has no designs on him.

"Alplaus." He smiles, then adds, "Upstate New York."

She nods, admits, "Never heard of the place. When did you get here?"

"Two days ago. We're leaving tomorrow."

We, she thinks.

"There's five of us."

"Five," she says. "Five guys? In one room?"

"No." He laughs. "Two. You save money that way."

They play their hands, and she lights up again, orders another beer.

"And you?" he asks.

"New York. City. I'm here with a friend. She must be somewhere, or up in the room."

He shakes his head at his cards. "I haven't won even one hand since I sat down."

"You've got to be patient," she says assuredly. "The cards will come, they tell you to be patient. I'm new to this game, but I totally love it. What's your name?" she asks, smiles at him. He doesn't drink, doesn't smoke, but is cute in a clean sort of way.

"Henry."

"I'm Maggie." She giggles. "I just remembered. I haven't eaten all day."

"As a matter of fact, I could eat something myself. We could go for a snack."

"A snack," she says, dreamily. She is pleasantly high, but her mind is clear. She doesn't feel like eating. She wants to win big, then she will eat. Her chips are dwindling, but she has more in her purse.

"Maybe later," she says. "If we leave now, we'll never get our seats back."

SHE IS LOSING A LOT. THE CARDS WON'T come her way. She is losing, losing. How did this happen? At one point, she was two hundred ahead, and then, somehow, gave it all back. How stupid she is, greedy. She should have left when she was ahead, but she wanted more, more. That's how they operate: they give you a taste, they suck you in, then suck you dry.

"I'll be back, please keep my seat," she tells the dealer in a low voice.

"Are you all right?" Henry asks, and it annoys her. It annoys her that he has remained at her side all night. He jinxes her; she plays differently because he is around.

She goes to the bathroom and enters the same stall, her familiar refuge. She could quit now and go upstairs, get a good night sleep.

No, she couldn't, she is not ready yet. She'd better hurry, or she'll miss a good hand. A four-of-a-kind. All night, she's been obsessing about four-of-a-kind. What time is it? They mustn't close the casino, they must give her a chance to win back her money. How badly she hankers for a four-of-a-kind: it will bring her back nicely. Persistence should be rewarded. And she has been persistent. Those guys upstairs who monitor the cameras may take pity on her and see to it that she gets a good hand.

Is she being ridiculous? Maybe, but everything is possible, she must believe in her luck.

Her hands are filthy from handling chips all night, and dirt has collected under her fingernails. She sits on the toilet and cleans them as best she can, wiping the dirt on tissue paper.

Who is she? she asks, gazing down at her naked thighs. Only losers like her possess this hardheaded stubbornness to win. She was so good yesterday, exercising self-control and going to bed early, at a normal hour. Then Robin had to come in and disturb her peace of mind. If it weren't for Robin, she wouldn't even be here, losing all this money and filling her body with alcohol and smoke. Susan was right: you'd better know who you're travelling with. And she had her doubts about Robin, and still, joined her on the trip, wanting to trust her. How naive she is, how blind, to have put her trust in someone like Robin.

She hears the click of high heels and comes out of the stall. A woman in a short black dress—so smooth and well cut, it hugs her curves—leans forward before the mirror and adjusts her breasts in her bra. How sophisticated she looks, Maggie thinks, staring at the deep cleavage, the exposed shoulders. She notes the diamond earrings and necklace, the deep, even tan, the crescent of light freckles just above the line of her breasts. She feels so small, unaccomplished, next to this polished blonde. Just look at those freckles—what a ravishing sight. If only she could be like her!

Before she can stop herself, Maggie hears herself say, "Oh, you look so nice."

"Thank you," says the woman with a broad, sexy smile. "I want to look nice."

An accent. Brazilian perhaps. A last, satisfied glance at the mirror, and the woman heads for the door.

"Have fun," Maggie calls after her.

"I hope so," says the woman.

Maggie studies her reflection. Take your time, she tells herself. Make yourself pretty. She'll put on lipstick. There. She is in no hurry to go back to the table. She is still in command, in full control of her compulsion. Gambling is not a priority, it's just a means, a pastime.

Back in her seat, she is staring at five cards—she has nothing, nothing. Staring at the cards won't change them. She'd better take her loss, put them down, wait for the next shuffle. She's run out of cigarettes. She has more in her room, but doesn't want to go upstairs. She spots a smoker who joins the table, and her spirits lift; she loves smokers.

She notices the Brazilian in the black dress sitting at a table across the aisle. An older, well dressed but tough-looking man is seated at her side. Obviously, a high roller. Men like him buy women gifts. Expensive gifts. She can tell they are together, but only for the night. She is not sure why she thinks that, but something in the man's manner, hard and matter-of-fact, tells her they are strangers to one another. But, if the woman sleeps with him tonight, he'll make it worth her while.

Again, her chips are dwindling. If her luck doesn't turn,

she'll have to go to the machine.

No, she's gone already a couple of times. She'd better go upstairs and call it a night.

But she is having fun, isn't she? And it's only money. If she goes upstairs, she'll never make her losses back. If she continues to play, she has a chance.

She tells the dealer to keep her seat, tells Henry she'll be back, and goes to the cash machine. It's only money, only money—the phrase, like a soothing mantra, keeps repeating in her head. She inserts her card.

No receipts are available, does she wish to proceed? the machine asks.

Oh, yes, she does.

She follows the instructions anxiously, punches her code number, the amount: one hundred. She waits, worrying that for some reason or other she won't be able to draw more cash.

Not to worry, she tells herself. She can always use her Visa card—she'll be charged a commission, but what the hell, she is enjoying herself.

Ah, what great relief: a crisp, one-hundred bill pops from the slot. What a neat idea, a cash-dispensing machine. How reassuring that while she is here, in the Bahamas, her life in New York still continues, on paper at least, and her wishes still command the respect of electronics. With more money, she is buying more time. It's a funny concept, that she is buying time. Ah, if only she could buy more time. The fact of the matter is that in a couple or so days she'll have to leave this paradise. The fact of the matter is that she is living on borrowed time, time grudgingly allowed her by a Mr. Faber. It's a distressing thought, that her time belongs to her boss. And to make things worse, so far she has drawn four hundred dollars she doesn't have: she has a thousand-dollar overdraft protection, and now she is four-hundred in debt. This is the absolutely last one-hundred: if she loses it, she'll go upstairs to the room, will go to sleep. Tomorrow is another day. She can recoup her losses tomorrow.

She goes back to the table feeling revived. She has a hundred dollars in her hand. Henry says something to her, but she has no patience to listen. With this one hundred, she'll make it all back, she knows she will. Four-of-a-kind is due to come. Or even a better hand—a straight flush, and she'll get ten percent of the jackpot: fifty-thousand bucks. It can happen. She must leave the table vindicated.

Vindicated? What's the matter with her? Whom is she fighting? The cards? The house? The dealers? They couldn't care less, or maybe they do, a little.

Better admit she's unlucky in cards. Unlucky, period. She is fighting her bad luck, but what makes her think she is entitled to win? Why should the cards come her way?

Because she is due, because she wants them to, because they will.

She isn't thinking straight, and no wonder. Except for breakfast, she hasn't eaten all day. She is ruining her health, drinking and smoking, but she has a mission, she must make it all back. Nothing waits for her upstairs, but an empty room. This is her first time in the Bahamas—her luck is bound to change.

Perhaps if she moved to another table.... This dealer, Pam, jinxes her.

Move? But she is so comfortable right where she is, her beer and water set up before her, her ashtray, and there's a smoker at the table she can bum cigarettes from. And she doesn't want the others to get the impression that she is no better than those desperate souls she feels sorry for, those who wander from table to table, losing some, then moving on. No, she'll stay put; she was meant to play at this table. Soon she'll get lucky, the odds are in her favor. This nonsense about Pam jinxing her is just utterly absurd, ludicrous. It's not the dealer, it's the cards; all she needs is one spectacular hand.

She hates this back and forth in her mind—it leads her nowhere, only confuses her more. She has not lost her head, has she?

Here, she won a hand—two-pair; small as it is, how it cheers her up, a winning hand. She'll yet make it all back, then will go upstairs feeling great, victorious. She can't leave now, feeling defeated, demoralized.

SHE'S LOST EVERYTHING. HER PURSE IS EMPTY. She is dragging herself upstairs, her heart, her pitiful heart, weighs her down. How could she let her mind trick her like this? Now her mind tells her she is pathetic, disgusting. Why didn't it tell her she is disgusting earlier? When she was ahead?

How miserable she'll feel the rest of her stay in this paradise. It's only her third night, and already she's ruined everything. Her only chance for salvation: stay away from the casino, no more gambling until the end of the trip.

But what will she do if she can't gamble?

It's all Robin's fault. Why wasn't she there to stop her? Already she dreads waking up tomorrow, mourning her losses.

She mustn't dwell on having lost so much, she must enjoy her vacation. It's only money. Somehow she'll manage, find a better-paying job, work with Robin for CBS.

If she ever speaks to Robin again.

In the room, too wired to sleep, she makes herself a drink. Robin, of course, hasn't come back. She said a couple of days, which means she might be back tomorrow. Robin in her lost red dress and her funky high heels, looking fabulous. And speaking of looks. She herself, she regrets to say, is a blurry image in the mirror above the commode. She can't even sit straight; she sits stooped over like a true drunk.

She lights a cigarette, and the room fills up with smoke. Again she tries to focus, find her face in the mirror. Such a fog in her brain. What is she doing to herself? She has no self-control. She's a shit, a monster, a wretched monster.

She drops ashes in her open purse, mistaking it for an ashtray. Ha! ha! the pits. She's so drunk, she has sunk so low—if only she could laugh. It's four o'clock in the morning. Why is she still sitting up and smoking? To prolong her misery? To delay the hour of waking? The turmoils she puts herself through, the emotional upheavals.

Tomorrow, she vows, she won't drink, won't smoke, she'll give her body a break. God, is she a loser! She was ahead at one time, and now she is back four hundred, plus the modest eighty she started with, and the two hundred she had won and stupidly gave back. Money that was in her purse for her to keep, and she gave it all back.

She hears water running in the bathroom. It must be what's-his-face, Henry. Why doesn't he go away?

She still has the three hundred dollars she came with, stashed away in the drawer. All is not lost. A deficit of four-hundred is still manageable. If she stays away from the casino, she'll be in good shape. She brought three hundred to lose, and lost four hundred. It could have been much worse.

IS SHE DREAMING? ROBIN AND WYNSTON, the security guy, are making out on the bed. Her bed. Look how they twist and turn, black against white. They're hot, they're sweating. His perfectly round skull, under the short-cropped hair, is gleaming with sweat. She is so shocked, so dazed, she can't even talk. So, he found Robin, and now he is fucking her. She always gets what she wants, doesn't she?—fucking, unreliable Robin. They're all unreliable. Why does she *trust* people? Why is she so needy?

Now he is kissing *her*. She is too tired to resist him so she kisses him back, somewhat disgusted. With him, with herself. It's no longer Wynston, for Wynston is black, and this guy is white, like sickly white. He gets on top of her and pushes at her cunt, then penetrates. She wants to cry. They are fucking now—the good, old, in-and-out business. So mechanical, so cold, so meaningless.

She opens her eyes. Light floods the room. Again she forgot to draw the curtains. It is not a dream. He is actually on top of her, moving like a piston.

She panics. "Wait," she cries, tries to push him off. But the bastard is off in his own world, he doesn't hear her. He groans, shivers, comes inside of her. Oh, shit, she thinks, horrified. Her eyes fill with tears, and she is numb with rage. How she hates the prick.

All at once she is frantic, she screams, "Let me up. Let me up," and he rolls off her.

"I'm sorry," he whispers, and she stares at him. It's that guy from last night.

"Fuck you," she screams. "The least you could do is use a condom."

"I know, you're right, I'm truly sorry. I didn't have one," he adds with a diffident smile.

God, she thinks, pushes off the bed. In the shower, she spreads her legs and bears down, watches his sperm drop to the floor in one, thick glob. So revoltingly pathetic, the sperm of men. She has only herself to blame.

She washes herself out. No real harm done. Her period is due in a day or two; he'll be washed out of her body. And AIDS? Not from this guy—he's too clean-cut.

She wraps a towel around her and goes back into the room. She is calm now, in control. He is fully dressed, sitting at the table near the veranda doors.

He stands up. He is so embarrassed, so *remorseful*, she wants to laugh. "Maggie," he says, takes a step toward her. "I'm truly sorry...."

"Don't." She raises her hand, and he retreats back to the chair. "I'm fine." At least he remembers her name. That's more than she can say for herself.

She lights a cigarette. "What happened?" she demands. "Last night."

"I brought you upstairs," he says, sitting down again. "You asked me to."

"I *asked* you to?"

He nods, smiles at her incredulity. "I swear. Then"—he waves his hand—"we just fell into the bed."

"Just like that."

He shrugs. "You were tired, Maggie, maybe a little drunk."

Haughtily, she smiles. A little drunk, sure thing. As if she would have fucked him sober.

She sits down on Robin's bed and looks around her. She seems to be missing something, but what? Oh, yes, her purse.

"Where's my—?" She stands up, sees her purse on the commode.

"It's right there," he says, following her gaze. "Nothing is missing. Except your girlfriend, of course."

She glares at him, trying to remember what she told him. "How do you know?"

"It's quite obvious." He smiles. "You're alone in the room."

"Are you suggesting that I lied?"

"I'm not suggesting anything." He seems alarmed by her tone. "You said last night that you came with a friend, and that she went off with some guys. But it's none of my business, I really don't care." He stands up. "Listen, my plane takes off in a couple of hours, but we could have breakfast together, if you like."

"No, thanks," she says, distractedly. "I appreciate it, though." She wants him to leave, is dying to look in her purse. She remembers going to the ATM machine, withdrawing money. How much? The figure four-hundred sticks in her mind. Or is it five-hundred?

"You seem worried," he says.

"I am." She looks up at him, as if he had just materialized in the room. She can see in his eyes that he is alarmed again. It's quite amusing, actually, the effect she has on him. What was she thinking about? Oh, yes, her money. She stands up and goes to her purse and opens it.

Just like she feared—it's empty. "Oh, God," she says and looks at him.

He seems embarrassed for her. "I know," he says, smiling nervously. "You lost a lot."

Why didn't you stop me, jerk? she wants to scream, but doesn't. Her mind goes blank and now she is all confused, unsure whom to blame.

"I can't believe it," she says, again looks in her purse, shakes it dejectedly, emptily, then drops to the floor and begins to sob. She gave back her winnings, and lost four-hundred more. She wails, "How could I do such a thing?"

"Here." He shoves a tissue between her hands. "Don't cry, please. Just stay away from the casino."

She cries even harder. Stay away from the casino? What is she going to do for the rest of the week?

"I can't afford to lose," she says between sobs. "I'm dead, dead. What was I thinking last night?"

"It happens to all of us."

"What am I going to do? Oh, God, I'm ruined." She pounds her fists on the floor.

"Maybe I could help," she hears him say.

"Really?" She looks up at him, blows her nose. "How?"

Shyly, he hands her a hundred-dollar bill. "That's all I can spare," he says, and she, wiping her tears, hesitates a moment then takes it.

"I feel awful," she says. "I want to pay you back."

"Don't worry about it." He looks at his watch. "I really must go. Are you going to be all right?"

She nods, gets up from the floor and follows him to the door. "Are you sure you don't want me to—?"

"Positive."

She shuts the door and leans against it. She looks at the hundred-dollar bill, then smiles. It's only a hundred, but it makes her feel better. A hundred is better than nothing. She'll hide it in the drawer with the three hundred dollars she came with. There's still hope, she's not totally broke. She'll have to pick up the pieces and go from there. She won't set foot in the casino. Not tonight anyway. Last night, she went a little overboard, it happens, she had a little fun, lost her head. She notices Wynston's card and tears it up, drops the shreds in the toilet and watches them float in the water, like tiny lost yachts. She concentrates her gaze on one of them and sees the people on deck, clinging to the rail and calling for help.

They must be seasick, Maggie concludes. And soon they'll drown. There's Robin, on her funky high heels. A lot of good they'll do her in the water as she struggles to breathe. Ben is nowhere to be seen; he must be busy, saving his own skin. Poor Robin—who would have thought she'd end up in deep water, gulping like a fish. Such an open, brilliant future, and now this.

Maggie shakes her head at the images she's just seen and leaves the bathroom. She opens the doors to the veranda and steps outside. What a nice breeze. And look at the very blue sky. It's the first time she's come out to the veranda. How quiet and peaceful it all seems from above.

So, Robin found a guy with a yacht and went sailing. Naturally, she wouldn't think of inviting Maggie to come along. Couldn't stand the competition? Or was she afraid that Maggie wouldn't fit in with Ben's sophisticated friends? Whatever it is, who cares? She can stand here and analyze Robin all day long, but what's the point? The truth is, she doesn't need Robin—by now, this fact should be perfectly clear. Robin has a problem, and it's not hers, it's not her worry: she has her own money problems to figure out. She'll brush her teeth, go down and have breakfast, then out to the beach where she'll swim, relax, read, repair the damage to her body. She has three more days, two more nights, and a room all to herself. Little scheming Robin won't stand in her way. Now that she is alone, she needn't fret about Robin. She can devote herself entirely to her own pleasures, her own needs.

SHE GOES DOWN TO THE BEACH, SEEKING comfort. She pulls a chair under an umbrella and sits down, leans her elbows on her thighs and gazes at the sand. Her chest is filled with smoke, and she imagines she must reek of liquor and nicotine. The dull thuds of a headache beat in her temples and she wants to gnash her teeth, to grind the acrid taste of alcohol out of her mouth.

She tries to avoid her thoughts, but they nag at her. How could she do this to herself? How could she put so much poison in her body? Maybe Tom was right, maybe she is an alcoholic.

She is thinking this, but doesn't really believe it. Normally, she doesn't drink that much. Only when she is out with people does she lose control. People make her nervous, that's her problem. In New York they are quick to label you an alcoholic if you drink a glass or two. Even so, as soon as she goes back home, she'll go to A.A. As a matter of fact, she can't wait to get home, go back to New York, be normal again.

She remembers the night before, and is filled with remorse, apprehension: disaster looms everywhere, only bad things will happen to her. She'll lose her apartment, will be fired from her job. She'll die young, from cancer, while everybody else will go on living, forgetting about her. She'll lose everything she has, and she hasn't got that much.

How pathetic she must have looked, making the trips to the ATM machine, marching with the resoluteness of a drunk. How well she can envision it, the kind of dogged, one-foot-at-a-time advance, her legs two heavy wooden logs, her brain heavy, fuzzy, yet still holding a beam of light to direct her onward.

She must soothe her bruised self. In her everyday life,

she reminds herself, she doesn't spend much. Not on clothes, not on food, she is pretty frugal—a habit with her. So, she allowed herself to go overboard last night. No permanent harm done, she won't do it again, she's learned her lesson.

This morning, thank God, she is the voice of reason. A good swim will cleanse her. Right this minute she feels too sluggish to make herself stand up and go into the water, but soon she will. She needs time to recuperate, gather strength and be herself again.

Here, she's up, she goes to the water, plunges in. Instantly, she feels renewed, revitalized. She'll repair all the damage her body suffered last night. How much better she feels now, talking away her anger, pain, frustration. She could blame the whole thing on Robin, but what's the point? Robin is not her appointed guardian.

Indeed, it's futile, but again she tries to recollect how she went from being two-hundred ahead to this four-hundred deficit; she can't remember going through six-hundred dollars. Maybe she dropped some money on the floor? Or left the money in the ATM machine?

Impossible, totally unlike her. She wasn't that drunk, was she? She drank a lot, but her mind was clear, she knew what she was doing.

What if she had a good hand, but failed to see it, being too tired and saturated with booze?

No way. Why dwell on this? Why torment herself even more?

At least the booze is free, even if she has to place a dollar-chip as tip on the waitress's tray. Last night, in tips alone, she must have spent twenty or more. It's a good thing they dilute the drinks—she can't imagine having drunk so much and made it up to the room.

She still has the three hundred cash she brought with

her, and the one hundred Henry gave her—here, she remembers his name, after all. This is the first time she took money
from a man, and a stranger at that. And why not? He slept in
her room, he used her body. And he is partially responsible
for her losses. She played foolishly, carelessly, wanting perhaps to impress him. What must he think of her? Did he like
her at all? He must have, he came up to the room with her.

She smiles, remembering how alarmed and remorseful
he looked. Tonight, she'll go down with two-hundred, but
tonight she'll play smart and quit when she's ahead.

Or maybe she won't. If she is really good, she must stay
in the room, watch TV, read, just take it easy. It's a good thing
she kept drinking water all night. No matter how drunk, in
some part of her brain, she still remembered what's good for
her, remembered she must take care of herself. And this is
important, taking care of herself.

She dives under, then floats on her back. How fit and
sound she feels in the water, the cool, sobering water.
Miraculously, last night's losses recede in significance: they
seem far and distant, a misfortune that happened to someone
else. She's in control again, on top of things; she's regained
her sanity.

As she swims in, she suddenly becomes aware of a shadow swimming right beneath her, perhaps some sea creature,
perhaps a large turtle. She panics, begins to swim faster to
get away from it, but the creature won't go away; stubbornly,
it keeps pace, following her. Should she scream, call for
help? She must, she must.

Just then she realizes it's her own shadow, the shadow of
her swimming figure, right there at the bottom, on the
smooth, golden sand. She almost laughs with relief, but is
still spooked by the shadow; there's something unpleasant,
even menacing, about it. She comes out of the water and

walks to her chair. Her own shadow. It amuses her to think that her shadow has come out of the water with her and must be as wet as she. How long has it been since she's seen her own shadow? As a kid, she saw it a lot, always looked for it, fascinated by this dark extension of herself. Now, walking to her chair, it still follows behind, tireless, extending from her body in a slant. She stands a moment and watches it. She likes what she sees: she looks taller, slimmer, like some dark African totem, carved in wood, graceful and mute and portentous.

Someone walks past, and she looks up. It's the old couple and their granddaughter. They smile at her and say hello, and she smiles back.

"What a beautiful day," says the woman, and Maggie nods. "We've been lucky with the weather," the woman continues. "Too bad we have to leave this afternoon."

Again Maggie nods; she can't think of anything to say. She gazes at the girl, a pretty blond angel with blue eyes and a small sturdy body. "What's your name?" she asks.

"Alice." The girl giggles and hides behind her grandma. One day, Maggie wistfully reflects, little Alice will grow up and men will invade her delicate frame, will force themselves between her thighs. Already, they must be eyeing her.

"Enjoy," says the woman, and the three of them continue toward the hotel.

Maggie goes over to her chair and buries her face in a towel. She shakes out her wet hair, just like so many actresses she has seen in the movies, standing on the sand on their tall shapely legs and shaking out their hair, a towel in their hand. She feels refreshed, restored. How nice it would be to sit on the beach, relax, sip a drink, smoke a cigarette. But she vowed she wouldn't drink, wouldn't smoke today. At least not until evening.

She wraps the towel around her and remains standing. Not too many people on the beach. Amazingly, most of the guests prefer the pool. There goes the waiter with his tray. She could call him over. No, she mustn't. And yet, her hand flies up and she is waving at him, and he waves back, gesturing he'd be right over.

She leans back in the chair and shuts her eyes, letting out a deep sigh. Henry, then Robin, cross her mind. Wait till she tells Robin about Henry. She'll say they fucked all night, that Henry went down on her and she came a dozen times. Poor Robin, who can't have orgasms, and who is stuck on a yacht with a middle-aged, balding beau.

Maggie realizes that she is smiling. In fact, she is happy. Or, if not happy, then pleased.

"What will you have?" The waiter bends over under the umbrella, creating an intimacy between them. It's the same boy who served them on the day they arrived. The same boy who couldn't keep his eyes off Robin.

"A beer, please." Her tone, she realizes, is a bit haughty, which is fine: she doesn't want him to get the wrong ideas just because she is alone. She doesn't want him to linger. "Any kind you have, and charge it to the room, please."

"Not a Bahama Mama?"

"No." She puts on her sunglasses.

A few minutes later, the waiter returns with a low plastic stool and, with much ceremony, puts down the can of Heineken on a napkin.

"Where are your friends?" he asks while she signs the check.

"In the casino." She hands him the check, barely contains her annoyance. He seems more forward today, more sure of himself.

"What about you? Don't you like to gamble?"

"Not very much." She sips the beer, is dying to light a cigarette, but not while he is there. What a nuisance, she thinks. What if others are watching, thinking perhaps she is the type to welcome the advances of a waiter?

She picks up her bag, pretends to be looking for something. She perceives herself through a third eye, and sees a woman alone, stingy with her time and affections.

"I'll leave you now," she hears him say. "If you need anything...."

"Thank you," she murmurs, still looking into the bag. She didn't mean to be rude, but how else could she get rid of him?

Melancholy is setting in; she'd better fight it, pull herself together. She lights a cigarette and inhales deeply, then picks up the book she's brought down to the beach. It's a novel by Dennis Cooper, a book she chose at the library with great care. The book will serve as a clue for that one special person who may approach her, may start a conversation. Cooper is cutting edge and so is she. Her tastes are. Even if, from looking at her now, no one would suspect it. She appears to be just another woman, sitting alone on the beach, reading a book. Such a sedate, ordinary picture. Such a deceivingly simple, one-dimensional life.

No one approaches her, no one bothers her, which is actually for the better. She cherishes the calm, the quiet. She should thank Robin, really, and maybe she will, if and when she sees her again. For even if they come back from their sailing trip, Robin will probably stay with Ben. For all she knows, Robin may even change her flight to accommodate Ben. Unless Ben tires of her, or she of him. Susan was right, saying you should only travel with someone close. And she, in her gullibility, said to Susan, Yes, we're close, we're good friends. Friends—such an imprecise, vacuous word.

Tears are rolling down her cheeks, but she feels too numb to wipe them off. She mustn't let Robin, or thoughts about Robin, ruin her vacation. And this guy Henry—they could have had a sweet night together, had she been sober. It's all her fault. Perhaps she shouldn't drink so much. But she likes to drink when she gambles, it's part of the fun. The smoking, the drinking, the sense that life is one, never-ending party. How is she supposed to control herself when she is having fun?

Never mind, never mind, she'd better concentrate on Cooper, and these two men, masturbating together. It overwhelms her, the way men make love to one another, so nakedly brutal and honest. None of the niceties and romantic pretensions, all the lies and sweet-talk of heterosexual love-making. In an earlier chapter, she read about fist-fucking. How intriguing, fist-fucking. What people won't do with and to their bodies. She herself is usually prudent, perhaps too prudent, when it comes to her body, to what she believes to be its well-being, her well-being. That's why it always amazes her, fascinates her, when others use their bodies as instruments for punishment and dissent. She wishes she could be as reckless as they, reach that higher plateau of absolute surrender, which, she so believes, must come from true desperation, from a true understanding of the world.

NAKED, SHE DANCES IN THE ROOM IN front of the full-length mirror. She drew a few puffs on a joint, and now is high, almost happy. Everything feels so pleasant; indeed, she is good at entertaining herself. If only this feeling could last forever! She shampooed her hair, and it smells so nice—she tips her head, pulls a few strands to her nose.

In the mirror, she is trim and lithe—not an ounce of fat on her slender rib-cage. She has the figure of a dancer, really. When she raises her arms up in the air, she can actually see her ribs. This fills her with wonderment, that such a primitive, elemental part of her anatomy would be so dangerously, so invitingly, exposed, so close to the surface. Reading Cooper, vicariously invading someone's asshole with Cooper's fist, filled her with the same kind of wonderment, of apprehension. Curiously, fist-fucking takes her back to childhood, reminding her of exploratory games children might play. They played all kinds of games, she and her friends. They played doctor and nurse, doctor and patient. They played grocer and customer, mommy and baby. And all with such serious devotion and innocence. Looking back, she can see herself at five, so absorbed in the game, in make-believe. This is what makes children so loveable, the earnest sincerity with which they approach everything. At moments of grace, like now, Maggie feels affection for that girl of five. She feels affection and mild sadness for this girl of twenty-six.

Still swaying with the music blasting from the radio, she massages body lotion onto her arms and legs, her breasts. Her ass. Her skin is nice and smooth. The idea strikes her that she can do what Cooper does, spread her cheeks to the mirror, explore her asshole. After all, it's hers, she's entitled to it. How fortunate she is to have a large hotel room with two double beds all to herself; she may do as she pleases.

She half-turns from the mirror, is prepared to bend over, but something stops her. Perhaps she shouldn't, it's too embarrassing. Yet, she completes the turn, bends over, spreads her cheeks to the glass.

A strange sight, not particularly appetizing, not to her anyway. She can't decide if it's beautiful or not, if she likes it or not. It is her body she is looking at, even if she can't recognize it, even if she views it as if it belonged to another. Years ago, her first boyfriend searched her vagina, using a flashlight. She just lay there on the bed, not even shy or amused, just indifferent, and let him look into her body. What is he looking for? she remembers wondering.

The telephone rings, and for a moment she freezes. Quickly, she straightens up, turns off the radio and picks up the receiver.

"Hello?" A man's voice. Allen? Searching for his lost Robin? "Wynston Foster here. From security. I'm calling to see if you're OK?"

Oh, the security man. The one who appeared in her dream. "I'm fine, thank you."

There's a pause on the line, and Maggie wonders if she sounds a bit out of breath—she stood up too fast, suffered a short dizzy spell.

"Have you heard from your friend, by any chance?" Wynston finally asks.

"My friend? Oh, yes, thank you."

"Is she all right?"

"Yes, she is."

"I'm glad to hear it." He sounds a bit surprised, perhaps relieved, but he is waiting for more. She must think fast: what will she tell him? She can't tell him that Robin abandoned her.

"She was called back on business," Maggie says. "An emergency."

"Really? Back to where?"

"Back home, New York. She works for CBS, you know, they always have some emergency or other. They're all incompetent, if you ask me. Anyway, you can stop worrying about her and take her name off the registration. It's just me in the room now."

"Well." Wynston pauses, digesting the news, and she gazes at the mirror, observes her breasts, her stomach, her pubic hair. Indeed, it is just she in the room now.

"Nothing left to say, I guess," Wynston says.

"I guess not." How strange that we should have pubic hair, she reflects. It serves no function. Some women shave it, maybe she will, too.

"Well, enjoy the rest of your vacation."

"Thank you very much."

She puts down the receiver. How easily she lied to this fellow Wynston. Her life, all things considered, is not as simple as it seems. A lot goes on in that brain of hers.

She brings her face close to the mirror. Not bad, not bad. Not a bad face. A bit flushed. Black, thick lashes, protecting her eyes, shading the brown irises. An all right nose, a full mouth, a slim body, definitely slimmer than Robin's. She is just as good-looking as Robin, if not more so. Obviously, it has to do with attitude. Outlook. Hers is all wrong, she must change it.

SHE WILL GO DOWN, AFTER ALL. SHE feels much better, almost normal. She'll go down for a while, play a little. If she's lucky, she'll make it all back. If she stays up in the room, her situation won't change. Staying in the room is like saying goodbye to her money. If she goes down, at least she's got a chance to get some of it back.

In the casino, she walks around the tables, studies the gamblers. The man with the cigar comes toward her and, smiling, she waves at him. He takes a moment, looking at her, and she fears he doesn't recognize her. But soon he does. "How you doing?" he says. "How'd you do last night?"

"All right," she says. "And you?"

"So-so. Good luck to you."

"I need it." She laughs, continues strolling. She's a bit anxious, is unsure which table to play. When she is ready, she must find a good one. Right now she feels gambled-out; she just wants to watch. In a little while, she'll take a seat, gamble with her head. That's why she came here. And to fuck her brains out, ha! ha!

Maggie smiles. The one guy who fucked her is now back in his living room. He gave her a hundred dollars, and she took it. Now he is entombed in snow, and she is here, in the casino, where beyond the sliding doors the night air is magically warm and caressing. She went out before, bought an ice-cream cone in the small mall. She window-shopped, licking ice cream and trying to feel touristic. It worked for a while, but pretty soon she was back in the hotel, her new home.

Here it is, her nemesis, the Caribbean Poker table. There's a vacant seat, waiting just for her. She tells herself not to, but pulls the chair and sits down, nods at the other players. The dealer greets her, changes her one-hundred-dollar bill into red, five-dollar chips, and white, one-dollar chips. She has two hundred more in her purse, but she won't touch it. Tonight she'll play intelligently. If she loses the one hundred, she'll quit.

"Good luck," says the dealer and places her chips before her.

"Thank you." She smiles, is all set to begin. Her heart is pounding, she remembers she must win.

"Any good hands?" she asks the table.

"Oh, yes," they tell her. The old lady seated at the end of the table hit four-of-a-kind an hour ago.

Four-of-a-kind! Maggie eyes the old, jeweled lady with envy, and resentment. Money goes to the moneyed. And they don't even need it. If she had got there earlier, she could have been the one. Four-of-a-kind would bring her back so nicely.

Very soon, her chips begin to pile up. It must be her lucky night. She orders a drink from the cocktail waitress— a glass of champagne, please. Champagne, they say, is good for you. And it's a classy drink. Yes, and now another glass. She's in business again. But tonight she'll keep a level head, won't let go of her winnings.

She is so good at managing her money. It's ten o'clock. She'll play till midnight, then go upstairs, read for a while, watch TV. Make it an early night, have an early start tomorrow.

"I'll be back," she tells the dealer and goes to the bathroom. She drinks and pees, drinks and pees. Her poor kidneys work overtime.

Coming out of the stall, she reminds herself about the new rule: she must take her time, make herself pretty. She glances in the mirror. She looks fine, quite attractive in fact. She doesn't need lipstick. She'd better hurry back to the table.

People come and go, faces change, but she, like the noise, is a constant presence. The casino should pay her, just for sitting there so long, attracting new faces to the table. Some of the dealers, she reflects, must know her by now. Do they discuss her when they take a break? Do they feel sorry for her? In their hearts, they probably feel contempt for all the losers they face, hour after hour, day after day.

She gazes at the machine that shuffles and deals the cards; the others watch it, too. It's a quiet table—nobody talks. It could be battle fatigue, or the particular personalities of those seated around her. Normally, it doesn't take much to bring a table to life. Maybe she'll do it, if she feels up to it.

More champagne for her, please. Another cigarette. One of the players—a young Asian—jiggles his chips, picking them up between his fingers and letting them drop, one on top of the other. It's a familiar sound that she's come to like, the casino sound of gamblers, their hands idle, their minds blank, waiting for cards to be dealt so they can pick them up and squeeze out their luck.

The dealer tells the Asian to stop jiggling his chips. It grates on her nerves, she says. Maggie is surprised, feels hurt for the guy. Probably a sailor. Many of them around here, so somebody said last night.

"Come on, give us good hands," she tells the dealer. "Wake this table up."

The dealer barely acknowledges her. The players, too, seem comatose. She is wasting her time. As a matter of fact, she doesn't like this table. Time to call it quits.

She cashes in her chips, counts her money. She is still in the running, has sixty dollars left. Playing all this time, she lost only forty—a bargain, but she hasn't had her fill yet. A few spins at the roulette table will set her straight. If she's lucky, she may double her money. Then she'll go upstairs and call it a night.

She checks her watch. Incredibly, it's past two o'clock, long past her designated bedtime. She can still manage a straight posture, but can barely keep her eyes open. She is tired and hungry. She could go upstairs, eat something, then come back down for a couple of spins. It's crazy, of course, but how often does she get to do this? She's on vacation, why not indulge herself, have a taste of the wild life? Everybody does when they're on vacation.

Upstairs, hunched over a towel on Robin's bed, she devours cheese and crackers from the robo-bar. She didn't realize she was that hungry. After breakfast, she had nothing all day. Not eating, she is saving time and money and is losing weight; she delights in the way her stomach lies flat against her hand—she is down to the bare minimum.

She makes herself a drink, lights a cigarette—she smokes up the room. Better open a window. No, the light will attract mosquitoes and other insects. Actually, she could easily fall asleep, lay her head on the pillow....

No, she decides, she will go down, but just for a little while. They say the best action is late at night.

She grabs her purse and leaves the room, goes down to the casino. It's much quieter now, only the serious gamblers are still at it. She walks around the roulette tables, hoping to spot a good one.

There—a good table, not too crowded, just four players, she is the fifth. They are four boisterous high rollers who cover all the numbers. She likes such tables, laden with chips. A lot of action.

"Give me a good color," she tells the croupier, lays down her sixty dollars.

"Give her a lucky color," says one of the guys. He smiles

at her, and she smiles back, liking him immediately. He is tall, handsome, he looks smart, fearless. He plays quarters— twenty-five-dollar chips—not scrimpy one-dollar chips as she does. Is he out of her league? She hopes not. If she wins big, she'll switch to nickels—five-dollar chips. He'll realize she is not one of those poor souls who come to the table with their very last dollar. He'll appreciate that, like him, she has money to burn.

"Hey, Chuck," one of the guys calls to him. "Throw me a couple."

Chuck—she appraises the name, watches Chuck as he tosses a couple of black chips to his friend. Money, she thinks, means nothing to these guys. They joke and laugh as they place their bets, sipping their drinks and puffing on their cigars. Men, by nature, are hustlers. They dare, they take action, the world is theirs. They're trained to go after things and possess them—women, mountains, whole continents. Why can't women, Maggie reflects with envy, be as free and boisterous? Why do they feel they must always be decorous, "feminine?"

She decides to play Chuck's numbers. Wherever he places a chip, she places one, too. She's on top of him—she smiles, glances at him. He is smiling, too, he must have noticed; an intimate moment at the roulette table.

34 comes out, a number she hates, never plays it. She looks to see if she is there. She is! They are. She won, thanks to him.

"Great," she says. "I never play 34."

The croupier slides her winning chips across the table: thirty-five bucks. To figure out how much Chuck won, she'd have to multiply thirty-five by fifty: he has two twenty-five-dollar chips on the number.

The cocktail waitress comes around, and Chuck turns to

Maggie, asks her what she'll have.

"Champagne," she says, and with a nod of his head he agrees with her choice. "Make it two," he tells the waitress. "The better kind." He places a chip on the waitress's tray.

A twenty-five-dollar tip! Maggie catches her breath. "And a glass of water," she adds quickly.

"Bottled," Chuck tells the waitress. "Where are you from?" he asks.

"New York," she says, trying to sound blasé, very much like Robin.

"Where about?"

"The Village."

"The Village," he repeats. "An artist?"

"An editor."

"Really. A film editor? Who do you work for?"

As she's about to correct him, saying, A book editor, not a film editor, she decides not to. "CBS," she says.

"Cool. You must be good."

She smiles. "The best."

He stares at her a moment, a hard, straight gaze, evaluating her, and she worries that he can see through her, through her lie. But then he smiles and begins to place his chips. She follows suit, notes his strong, muscular arms. Exactly the type of man she, or any other woman, would want for herself. Much better-looking than Ben, or any of the men Robin ever laid her chubby paws on.

SHE NO LONGER BELONGS TO HERSELF. As they come at her with the rhythmic motion of waves. It's happening down below, in a different section of her body. She feels pain, but the pain is so remote, it seems inconsequential. What matters to her is the steadiness of movement, it mustn't stop.

Now a new guy enters her body, and the pounding resumes. On top of her, a man is breathing: she is the source of his pleasure. She, too, is breathing, moaning. A woman moans in the act of love, doesn't she? Did the first one come? Or did he give up on her? She wants him to come, he must come.

She is lost in her head, but she will persevere. She is performing a duty, just like any other duty—it's part of the contract.

What contract?

She tears her eyes open to count them. Her eyes hurt, and it is difficult to see. They are dark, hulky shadows against the wan light. Could they be three? Four? How did they all get in? Who gave them the key? She can't remember letting anyone into her room.

She shuts her eyes, she is beat. Let them finish their business and go. After they leave, she'll sleep some more, then wash them out of her body; it's that simple. She'll have breakfast, then go swimming. How many more days, nights, has she got left? It doesn't matter, she doesn't want to think about it. But she'll be sad, very sad, when her vacation is over. She always is.

She wakes up with a headache, sits stunned on the bed. In a flash she remembers. The guy from the roulette table. The one who got her the good champagne. The handsome high roller playing quarters. Chuck they called him, and he seemed to be their leader. Guys always have a leader. Did she invite him up? She must have. Did he let the others in? Possibly. She has a vague notion that he shouldn't have, but what can she do? Who can she complain to? She has no proof, no evidence, no clear memory. Her body is the evidence, but the alcohol count in her blood is evidence as well. She mustn't call attention to herself, or they'll kick her out of the hotel. She can't run downstairs and whine to Wynston about four guys who raped her. Was it rape at all? As it is, Wynston already must have his doubts about her. She would, too, if she were in his shoes.

What would they call it? Consenting adults. Adults. She is an adult. She'll wash out her cunt and go down for breakfast. Have a hearty one. She is ravenous, physically and mentally. She has endured a lot in the last few days, has expended a lot of energy. She must be good to her body, sustain it. Her stomach feels so empty, it sticks to her back.

The room is a mess. Except for a small crack, the curtains are drawn. Those fellows were smart, thinking ahead. The covers of both beds are on the floor. Who else was fucking on the other bed? Whoever it was, she must believe she was the main attraction.

She gets off the bed and drags herself to the bathroom. Her bones ache, but her life still continues. In the shower, she spreads her legs wide open. Her thighs feel sticky. She washes herself out, marvels at the fact that her cunt, having taken so much, is supple and velvety as ever.

She should feel a little weirded out, shouldn't she? Well, maybe she should, but she doesn't. You can't force these things. You either feel weirded out, or you don't. The way things stand now, she can outlast them all.

Perhaps, she reflects, this is how Dennis Cooper feels about his hole.

Several used condoms in the wastebasket. Good boys,

she thinks, good boys.

In the room, she finds her purse—it feels heavy. Amazed, she opens it: it is filled with chips. Not white dollar chips, but lots of greens and reds, and seven black chips. She must have done extremely well last night. She played his numbers, she remembers that—they must have been on a roll. She chose wisely, didn't end up with a loser.

She empties her purse on the bed and sits down to count the chips. A thousand bucks! She doesn't remember having won that much, but the money is in her purse, it belongs to her, she must have won it somehow.

She stops for a moment to consider, "somehow." Something nags at her, but it's so vague, she won't make the effort to grasp it, she must shrug it off. Why let doubts trouble her mind?

She hides the money in a drawer and leaves the room, goes down to have breakfast. All at once, she feels light and cheerful in her bathing suit, her T-shirt, her colorful thongs. She has cash, lots of cash, she's way ahead, she can afford anything her little heart desires. Her little heart! It desires a lot. And how good she feels. As one is supposed to, on a true vacation, not having to count one's pennies. She loves this island. If only she could remain in this sunshine forever.

The black maitre d' pulls a chair for her, and she smiles brightly, unfolds the napkin over her lap. It pleases her that he recognizes her, that he knows who she is. He stoops slightly and pours water into her glass, asking, "How are you this morning?" She is fine, fine, couldn't be better. This is the life. Being served breakfast in a luxury hotel. Have others defer to you, your pleasure their business. If only Robin could see her now.

"It's such a beautiful day," she says to the maitre d', and he smiles, bows again and says, "Indeed, it is."

"I was very lucky last night," she tells him. "I did well in the casino."

"Really?" His face lights up. "I'm happy for you." He remains at her table, straightening out the starched table-cloth, and now she worries she was too friendly. "My fiancé," she says, "may join me in a day or two."

"Let's hope that he does." The maitre d' smiles. "Enjoy your breakfast."

"Thank you."

Food is placed before her, and she devours it. God, she is hungry. Ah, the comfort of a soft-boiled egg, done just right. Here they serve it in a small glass bowl, but her mother used to serve it in an egg-cup, and she would crack the top and peel the shell then dip her spoon. How she loved the whole ritual, how she loved her mother, sitting next to her, peeling a tomato and spooning out the pulp for her little daughter.

Her mother. If her mother can see her, Maggie hopes her mother doesn't worry about her. She is doing fine, and will be doing even better, she can feel it in her bones. She's becoming stronger, bolder, is in full command. More toast, please. And yes, more coffee. And now jelly, to leave a sweet taste in the mouth.

A FTER BREAKFAST, SHE GOES UP TO THE ROOM. The room is still a mess, and the red message button is blinking. How long has it been blinking? She hasn't noticed it before. She picks up the receiver, presses down the button. She has one recorded message, says the machine. Would she like to listen to it? Yes, she would, please. Dial one, says the machine, and she does. A few clicks, and Robin is on the line, so close, so accessible. "Hi, sweetie, it's me. You'll never guess, but we're somewhere"—Robin laughs—"we're sailing to Miami. Anyway, our plans changed and we won't be coming back. I guess I'll fly home from Miami. I really hoped we'd spend some time together, but the gods willed otherwise. Please don't be angry, I'll explain everything when I see you in New York. And, I promise, I'll make it up to you. Dinner on me in a restaurant of your choosing, all right? Hey, Mag, have fun, you hear? It's an order. Did you find my red dress? Love you." Another click and Robin is gone. Would she like to listen to the message again? Yes, she would. Here's Robin's sweet voice again. How cheerful she sounds, without a care in the world. Lucky Robin. She always gets what she wants. Would she like to listen to the message again? Yes, she would. She listens, listens. *I really hoped we'd spend some time together*. How much does it cost to say the right words? Not much, apparently. Would she like? asks the machine. Yes, she would. She listens intently. She's on a merry-go-round with Robin's voice. Round and round they go, there's no beginning, no end. Robin's reddish hair blows in the wind. Such a pretty picture, such a pretty child. Without a care in the world. Love you, Robin says. Love you, love you.

Love you, sure. Love you, too, Robin, love you too.

Maggie erases the message and puts down the receiver. She lies down on the bed and shuts her eyes. She is not even surprised that Robin is off to Miami. For all she knows, Robin may stay there forever, or follow Ben wherever he goes. No, she is not surprised. Somehow she knew it all along. This is Robin for you: spontaneous, living the moment. No consequences, or other people, considered.

She feels tired, she'll take a little nap. It's ridiculous to take a nap at eleven in the morning, but why not? Her body demands it. She loves this kind of life where the hours don't count, but obeying your whims does.

She drifts away, existing nowhere. She is startled to hear someone snoring beside her. She opens her eyes, realizes it must have been she who snored. Tom was a big snorer. In the middle of the night she would kick him, with pure hate, to make him stop. Incredibly, he never woke up, never had to face her hatred.

A knock on the door. It must be the maid. "Come in," she calls, and indeed, Sophia appears in the room. How she is glad to see her!

"Hello, Sophia." Maggie sits up. "How are you?"

"Fine, Miss. And you?"

"Very fine. Come in, come in, you may clean up. I'll get out of your way in a sec."

She leans on her elbow and regards the maid. There's something about this woman that appeals to her. There's something about this woman that she likes. Likes a lot. "How are you, Sophia?" she asks, remembering she's just asked her this question.

"Fine, Miss."

Maggie jumps out of bed. "What do you think, Sophia? What do you think I should do? Go to the beach or the casino?"

Sophia, a bit embarrassed, smiles. "I don't know, Miss."

"That's it, Sophia." Maggie laughs—she feels so happy and doesn't even know why. "I don't know either, you see, I can't make up my mind." She looks at herself and at Sophia through the mirror. "I have something for you, Sophia," Maggie whispers, and the maid's eyes widen, not understanding. "Something beautiful," Maggie whispers conspiratorially. "Maybe not for you exactly. Do you have a daughter?"

Sophia nods, Yes.

"Great." Maggie goes to the closet and brings out the red dress. "I want you to have it. Here, take it, it's yours."

But Sophia is reluctant, which surprises her. Unless, of course, the maid is overwhelmed by the splendor of the dress, which makes sense.

"I don't know, Miss."

"Trust me, Sophia, it's all right, you have nothing to worry about."

"But my daughter"—the maid gestures that her daughter is large, and it seems to Maggie the maid is lying.

"Then you must have a niece—don't you have a niece?"

Sophia nods.

"There you go. Don't give me a hard time, Sophia, I like you, you know that, don't you?"

"Yes, Miss."

"Let me find a plastic bag for you. It's a beautiful dress, as you can see, one hundred percent silk." She puts the dress in a bag and hands it to the maid.

"Thank you, Miss," Sophia says, blushing under her dark skin.

"You're very welcome. Now, don't mind me, Sophia, you go ahead and clean."

Sophia obeys. She goes to Robin's bed and begins to pull off the sheets.

"Oh," Maggie says. "It's a real mess in here this morning, isn't it? I never sleep in this bed." She points at Robin's bed. Now she remembers the condoms in the wastebasket. "My friend slept here last night, but she went back to New York early this morning. She didn't like it here."

"No?" says Sophia.

"No. Some problem with men. She couldn't take it, so she left. No place like home, as they say. It's better this way, I think. What do you think, Sophia?"

"Yes, Miss."

Yes, Miss. She could go into the bathroom and cover the condoms with tissue paper. She could, yes, but she doesn't want to. She'll go down to the beach, that's what she'll do. The real casino action only begins at night.

SHE STARTS THE EVENING SLOWLY, deliberately. It is her last night, and she wants it to last. Last. In her purse she has a couple of black chips; the rest of her money is safely stashed away. Tonight, she'll play craps, she hasn't played craps since she got here. The crowds at the crap tables are rowdier, perhaps a bit crude, but some of the players are high rollers, and she likes high rollers, their easy manner, their pinky diamond rings. The casual way they handle their money, their women. Shrewd and hard, they seem to know the true nature of life, of people: they know and manipulate the ways of the world. This is the kind of knowledge she feels she lacks and must acquire, fast, in order to succeed. With success on your side, and cash to back you up, you can show your true colors, never having to pay any mind to what others may think. She always worries too much, wants to be and make nice. How tiresome and, ultimately, futile. It is time she joined the other camp, the camp of the doers, the

camp of the ruthless. All it takes is resolve, never losing sight
of the ultimate goal.

Like a predator, she stalks the crap tables, watching,
observing. She is in no hurry. Eventually she'll find what she
is looking for.

Her stomach is nice and full, she has treated herself to
dinner at a restaurant in the mall. She chose like a true con-
noisseur: first course, conch salad; second course, grouper "à
la Creole," and for dessert, a guava puff, served deliciously
warm. Sipping her chardonnay, she lit a cigarette, then casually surveyed the diners around her. To her pleasant surprise
she didn't feel intimidated being alone. In certain respects,
she was superior to them, managing on her own. All the others were couples, of course, but that was to be expected.
People flock to the sun for their bit of honeymoon. She and
her ex did. They went to Aruba. Both rituals were performed
as if by rote: they got married, they went on a honeymoon.
That's what most couples do. Later, as often happens, they
got a divorce.

It was unconscionable, Maggie thought, how young
women were duped into the moon-and-honey deal. Sipping
her chardonnay, she wondered how long it would take before
the flushed brides at the neighboring tables would find
themselves, one sultry night, masturbating next to the heavy
mass of their sleeping husbands. Just as she did, so long ago.
She could have masturbated on the couch in the living room,
but something drove her to do it right next to him, a sort of
defiance and vengeance brewing in her. At times she wondered if perhaps he lay there, listening, as her breathing
turned quick and shallow and she twitched on the bed in her
solitary pleasure. Day and night she considered divorce, but
never dared to utter the word. It was he who finally suggested divorce—perhaps to test her, perhaps hoping she'd say

no, but she said yes.

Observing the other diners, she wondered how many of them would remain married, and for how long. She had learned too soon to be cynical about love, and yet, she thought it sad, tragic, that people who loved each other one day, should hate each other so vehemently the next. She recalled one particular night when she and Tom were in bed, preparing to fall asleep, and she snuggled up to his wide back and vowed in her heart never to leave him. Two years later they were divorced.

One of the crap tables erupts; players give each other the high five. She approaches. Looks like a good table. A bit crowded, but a lot of action. The shooter has just rolled a winner—his fourth. She can join the game now, it's a new come-out roll. She finds a spot at the table, buys chips, places a five-dollar chip on the Pass Line. The shooter, an older man in his seventies, shakes the dice in his hand, then blows on them.

This guy is good, she decides. An old timer. He knows what he is doing. Too bad she wasn't in it from the start.

Seven! Again the table erupts. Way to go! Everybody gets paid. "Roll as many sevens as you like!" someone shouts. "Get them out of your system."

"Keep going," shouts another. They are merry. She, too, is merry. This is the life, she is winning.

"Give me a horn bet," she shouts, tosses a five-dollar chip on the table. The shooter rolls a two. Now they're all quiet, shifting their weight on their feet, keeping a lid on their disappointment. They all lose their Pass Line bet, but she wins the horn bet. Not bad, she thinks, aligns her chips. Let him keep rolling. When her turn comes, she will be the shooter. She wants to roll numbers, a couple of elevens, a couple of winners. Then the players will love her, will consider her one of their own. They will smile at her and cheer her on, gladly granting her a moment of glory. Some of them may find it sexy, the way she rolls the dice and keeps winning for them all. Yes, sexy, she wants to feel sexy, desired.

But when her turn comes, she fizzles out very fast. "Come on, shooter," someone calls to her, and she smiles, pitches the dice across the table. One of them flies high and over, nearly hitting a player at the other end. They all laugh goodhumoredly, and new dice are put before her. She picks two, shakes them a moment, delighting in the way they feel in her palm, then shoots. Eleven! Her favorite win, but she forgot to play the horn bet. Still, all of them get paid on the Pass Line. Again she shoots. A five. That's the number she'll have to shoot again before she rolls a seven.

She hates five. She has a premonition she won't roll another, but she must be positive—it's all in the dice.

"Come on, thirty-two," someone shouts.

"Remember your number, shooter," someone else shouts, and she throws the dice. An eight. Not bad. She doesn't play eight, but others do, they get paid thanks to her. More players put money on other numbers, trusting her.

"Way to go, shooter," they yell, and she picks up the dice, hurls them across the table. Unbelievably, it's a seven—her heart sinks. She stares at the dice, unwilling to accept that her turn is over, and so soon. Instantly, attention is taken away from her—she is nothing, she is just another loser. They were willing to bet their money on her, and she failed them.

Crestfallen, she turns from the table, walks away with a heavy heart. She should have remembered her number, just like the man said. She should have concentrated on five, should have willed it. Instead, she jinxed herself, lost confidence in her number and shot the dice as if her hand didn't belong to the rest of her. She'll have to go back and try again later, redeem herself. She'll focus harder, throw the dice with real determination.

Someone bumps into her, snaps, "Watch where you're walking, lady," and she is so shocked, she just stands there, in the middle of the casino floor, and watches the fucking asshole hurrying ahead.

"You bumped into me, you jerk," she wants to scream after him, but what's the point? Oh, if only she could hurt him in some way, hurt him where it really hurts.

Why is she so enraged? Because. She'd love to run after him and punch him in the face, kick him in the groin, the lower back. Men take advantage of their physical strength, their supposed superiority, but only with women. He'd never dare use this tone and language with another man. Unless he were asking for trouble.

A sore loser, she concludes. Let him lose some more.

SHE IS HOLDING CARDS IN HER HAND, IS unsteady on the high stool. What is she playing? Caribbean Poker. That's right. Caribbean Poker.

Poker. What a funny name. Her mind is dead clear, but it crawls like a giant tortoise, slow and heavy. She loves poker, loves poker players. Poker crystallizes the moment, focuses the mind. A couple of men at her side. Either side. They order drinks for her, are attentive to her needs. It pleases her that they're attentive to her needs. Men sometimes are so sweet, so nice to women, she could cry.

Her head feels light on her shoulders, which is good, very good. She's been sitting here for a while, God only knows what time it is. They're having lots of fun, they're laughing all the time. She and the guys. The dealer is sour-faced, begrudging their joy. What's his problem, she wonders. Is it her fault? She's been losing a lot, but who's counting? She is having fun, the rest is irrelevant. The cards tonight are against her, but her chips, magically, never run out; her pile keeps replenishing itself.

She giggles. It must be the man on her left. Or the man on her right. Which one? It doesn't matter. They're both equally sweet. Gentle. Generous. Out to have a good time.

"Hey," she wants to shout. "We're all human. Let's make the most of it."

"Let's make the most of it." Here, she's said it. She slurs her speech, but so what? A hand caresses her back, and the guy on her right says in her ear, "Yes, baby," and her ear tingles with his voice.

Yes, baby. She wants to rest her head and hear it again. Baby. She likes to be called baby. So much affection in one little word. They could go up to his room, but no fucking, please, just lying down together, just being nice.

He said, "Yes, baby." Did she ask him a question?

"Did I ask you a question?" she asks, tries to look into his face. His face is a blur. She blinks a couple of times, she laughs—it's too funny, her eyes won't focus. It's a miracle she can still see her cards.

She hears laughter. They laugh. Which is good. She, too, laughs. She likes to laugh. What's better than laughter? They're discussing different brands of cigarettes and the guy on her left says he'd smoke any brand. "As long as it burns," he says, "I'll smoke it."

"Me too," she shouts, then covers her mouth, giggling.

More laughter. She has a sense that he is a big guy, not at all her type, but he is funny; she feels drawn to his masculine buoyancy.

A hand goes under her shirt, a large, virile hand on her bare skin, whose touch sends a spasm down her spine and fills her with longing. She wants to cry. Her head fills up with memories, she is drowning in memories. Not the memories themselves, but the notion that memories exist, like this one, which idly, as if by command, surfaces—funny that this particular one does. It's amazing how clearly she can see it, she's about seven or eight years old and she stands in the open field on a hot day and watches the neighborhood boys play baseball. She is watching the game and this man comes up to her and tells her that his niece, who is new in the neighborhood, is visiting; would Maggie go with him and play with his niece? Maggie wants to say no, she wants to watch the game, but doesn't want to appear impolite, so uncaring about the niece. Reluctantly, she goes with him, and they arrive at his house. A couple of women stand at the curb, and Maggie feels vaguely ashamed for being seen with the guy.

In the house, he tells her to stand by the window and watch out for the niece who should arrive momentarily. Maggie stands by the window, feeling stupid, bored. The man comes to the window and leads her to the floor and they sit down. Now she notices that the room is empty of furniture. The man tells her that her fanny is smudged, here, he'll clean it for her. She is burning with shame. He is sitting behind her and pulls down her shorts and with a wet finger begins to rub her fanny. She doesn't remember how long she sat there, but some time later he got off the floor and said that his niece didn't show, and that Maggie could go home. She went home, but was too embarrassed to tell her parents about the man. Now she wonders how she knew to be embarrassed. Now she wonders if he rubbed her with his finger or his penis. She doesn't remember pain, so, at least, he had the decency not to penetrate her. There were a couple of other incidents she kept secret, like the time she played hide-and-seek at a friend's house. The friend's father was lying in bed, and he invited Maggie to come and hide under the covers, and Maggie jumped in, excited about this new hiding place where her friend would never think to look. Then the father took her hand and placed it on the warm flesh between his legs, and Maggie knew he was doing something forbidden. His wife and daughter were right there, only a few feet away, and Maggie's own parents were in the house next door. Again, Maggie felt strangely ashamed, and yet awed, and she writhed out of her hiding place, resumed playing with her friend, and after a couple of minutes said she had to go home. She didn't tell a soul, not her parents, not her friend, knowing it would only cause trouble. But how did the father know she wouldn't tell?

She is shaking, she is freezing. Why is it so cold in here? Is it cold, or is it her? She may be hungry; it's been a while since she's had dinner.

"Excuse me," she says to the dealer, "I must go to the bathroom."

"Don't forget to come back," one of the guys says.

"No, no," she coos, "I won't."

She makes her way to the bathroom, one foot in front of the other, sometimes too much in front, and sometimes sideways, as if she were performing some kind of a spasmodic ballet. Which makes her laugh. She is finally dancing—the cha-cha-cha or the tango. A solo performance for a select and privileged audience.

In the stall, she locks the door, sits down and searches

her purse. She finds a couple of crackers, and proceeds to devour them. As she chews, she becomes aware of herself and is amazed that she is doing this, sitting like this in a bathroom stall, munching on crackers. They dry out her mouth, but fill her stomach. She'll have some water when she goes back to the table.

In front of the mirror, she cleans her teeth with tongue and finger; it's an ungainly sight to have food sticking to your gums. At least she is sober enough to remember she cares about how she looks. She sniffs her armpits—the sweet scent of her body. She likes the way she smells, and men, apparently, like it, too. No one ever complained about her odor except for Tom. It irks her that she believed him, that she began to worry about her odor. Let him see her now, living her life, big time. Yeah, big time.

She looks at herself. Tonight she is wearing a tight-fitting, black T-shirt, and black, French cotton pants. She looks OK, but her outfits are all wrong. Fucking Robin, telling her what to pack.

She marches back to the table, to the two guys who are waiting for her.

"It's a real pain," she tells the dealer. "Why is the ladies' room always farther away than the men's? It's not fair."

"Shhh." Laughing, the man at her side leans toward her, his hand caressing her back. "Not so loud."

"Loud?" she says. "Am I loud?"

"Yes," the man whispers. "They don't like it when you're loud."

"Oh." She giggles. "We mustn't be loud, we must follow the rules. Am I winning?" She attempts to count her chips.

"You're doing all right," says the guy. His hand is on her back, under the shirt. He unfastens her bra.

Again, she tries to look into his face. "It's against the

rules," she whispers in his ear, and they both laugh. She feels witty, smart, worldly.

"Do you like my odor?" she whispers.

"Oh, yes," he whispers back, rubs his nose against her neck.

"Tom, that's my ex, was a real jerk. He didn't like my odor."

"Really?" says the guy.

"I came with a friend, you know, but she had to go back to New York. Some urgent business."

"We won't miss her." The two guys laugh.

"She is very pretty," Maggie says.

"Not as pretty as you," says the guy on her right, and Maggie smiles, gives a little shrug of the shoulders.

"Maybe not," she says, laughing with them. "The truth be told, I'm glad she's gone, she's a real bore sometimes. I mean, she is nice, but she's a bore. You know what she told me?"

"Shhh, not so loud, you can tell us later."

"She likes to call me sweetie. Sweetie here, and sweetie there. It's so phony, it makes me sick just to hear it. But I never tell her to stop, I don't want to hurt her feelings. Imagine, her feelings." Maggie laughs.

"Shhh," says the guy. "Not now, baby, later."

IS IT MORNING AGAIN? AGAIN SHE FORGOT to draw the curtains, but never mind, she wants to get up, why waste her life, sleeping? She pulls herself out of bed and looks for her purse. It is filled with chips and with one-hundred-dollar bills. Again, she's done well last night. She gets her money out of the drawer and counts it all.

She likes to count money, lots of it. All together, nearly two thousand bucks. She's never held so much money in her hand; she'll be going home with a bundle. Home? Is today her last day? Yes, it is, she'd better start thinking about packing. But she doesn't want to think about packing, she feels too mellow to think about anything. Maybe she is wrong, maybe it's not today, maybe it's tomorrow?

She gets her ticket from the drawer and studies it. For a moment she panics: she missed her flight. No, she didn't, it's at two p.m. And even if she were to miss it, so what? There are many other flights. Why must she leave today? Because she has a ticket with a date on it? Dates can be changed. She may be penalized, but she has the cash to cover it. She could easily stay for a couple more days, God knows she could use the rest. Besides, it will be silly of her to leave now, at the height of her success. She can call the office and tell them she fell ill, she can't fly home in her condition. Which is close to the truth: she doesn't feel like exerting herself this morning. And if Mr. Faber decides to fire her, good riddance, he'd be doing her a favor. She'll get unemployment and look for another job. And if her luck in the casino holds up, she won't even need to worry about a job. At least not for a while.

Can she stay? Yes, she can. The more she thinks about it, the more plausible it becomes. She must stay. It is only now that she has begun to enjoy herself, she is not ready yet to go back and face her life. She'll call the front desk and tell them she is sick, something she ate at the hotel, maybe food poisoning? She will pay for her room, in advance, and in cash, they will like that. Look at all the money that fell into her lap—the powers that be want her to stay.

She lies down on the bed. She must make up her mind. If she doesn't stay, she must hurry and pack, have breakfast, take a cab to the airport. But she doesn't want to leave in a hurry. When she's good and ready to leave, she'll do so slowly, leisurely. What's the point of a vacation if you have to hurry and hassle at the very end?

She sits up, counts her money again. She's done well last night, and there are more nights to come. So, she's made up her mind. A couple of phone calls, and she'll be all set. How easy, and simple. All it takes is making the right decision, and she has just made it. For the time being, she'd better do something with the money. Maybe open a bank account, or put it in a safe. They have everything she needs in the hotel. Last night, she and the guys bought condoms in the all-night store. How they laughed and roared in the elevator because in the store she had said, "Why condoms? We don't need condoms, I just want to cuddle." She wasn't joking, she tried to tell them, but they were laughing so hard, she couldn't help herself, she laughed, too.

Momentarily, this memory about the guys clouds everything, but soon the cloud lifts and she is herself again.

She goes into the shower, stands still under the stream of water. Blood is dripping down her thighs. Alarmed, she stares at the blood, and is then relieved. Her period. Her good, old period. It's amazing that her body, in spite of everything, keeps going. Like clockwork.

The long trace of blood zigzagging down her leg is a beautiful red, a shimmering trail originating from her cunt.

She is alive, bleeding from inside, like any other healthy female.

She cleans herself out, turns off the water. It's another reason to stay put. On the first day of her period, she has cramps and feels a bit out of sorts. Definitely not the ideal disposition for flying home. And what's the hurry? She has all the time in the world, she can afford to take a break.

All the time in the world. What a lovely expression. She is master of her own time, her own body. The lawful owner of both.

After breakfast, she'll go down to the beach, repair the damage of excess liquor and nicotine. She will lie in her chair and read, give her body a rest. She is operating on a system of her own devising. Abuse and repair is her modus vivendi.

THEY'RE DOING HER HAIR, HER NAILS, her toes. One girl at her feet, painting her toes; one girl at her side, massaging her hand before doing her nails; and yet another works on her hair. Her eyes shut, she is but a body now, abandoning itself to the care of others. How comforting, how pleasant to be treated like this. All her senses are alert and passive at the same time. She probably looks just like the guys she's seen through barber-shop windows in New York: the barber cuts their hair, a manicurist does their nails, and a shoe-shine boy shines their shoes. Some of them top the effect with a fat cigar sticking from their mouths. When she looked at them through the window, she thought how decadent they looked, how vulgar, but now she understands the logic of it, the logic of saving time, the logic of letting yourself get the full treatment. And why not? If you can pay for it. And she can. She feels grand, actually, letting herself be handled. And, she's in good hands: these girls are professional, trained to please and heighten the experience of their customers while tending to their needs. How they fuss about her, telling her how pretty she looks with her new hair. "Look in the mirror," they say, and she obeys, tries to connect with her new image. Her face is so different, she can hardly recognize it; it'll take some adjusting to get used to it. Her hair is a metallic blond, and it sits on her head like a heavy helmet. "Do you really like it?" she asks the girls uncertainly, and they say, "Yes, yes, you look wonderful." All right, then, she looks wonderful. And her nails and toes are bright red—how nicely they offset her tan skin. And to think that she used to hate nail polish! How foolish and immature of her old self.

"You know," she tells the girls. "A guy once drove me home from Atlantic City. I went there with a friend, but she decided to stay a little longer. She met a guy, you see." Maggie sort of laughs, and the girls smile and nod their heads. "Anyway, I missed my bus, but I met this guy at the poker table and he offered to give me a ride. I was a little afraid, you never know in New York, but he was very gentle and polite, and all the way home he told me about his life." She pauses, reminiscing. "He had been married three times and had grandchildren. He said that women loved him because he loved them. He was a professional gambler."

"Really?" say the girls. They stand there and look at her, expectantly.

"Yes." She contemplates them. He also told her he liked

to frequent a movie theater on West Street and let a man blow him. But what about the other guy? she had asked, more out of fear than real interest. What's his pleasure? And the man said that giving a blow-job was the most beautiful thing one human being could do for another, and Maggie wondered if he truly believed that, or was insinuating perhaps that she might want to do the same for him.

"Well." Maggie sighs. These girls may misunderstand if she begins to talk about blow-jobs. She strokes her hair. "Thank you very much. This is exactly what I wanted."

DENNIS COOPER IN HER LAP, SHE SITS ON the beach, looking out at the water. She has discarded her old-fashioned swimsuit from New York and bought a new one, to go with her new hair. It snakes along her body in yellow and red stripes, and sits high on her hip bones. True, it's a bit too tight, and it cuts unpleasantly into her skin, but it does showcase her legs to great advantage. "It's not too flamboyant?" she asked the salesgirl in the shop, and the girl said, "No, not at all, it's the latest style."

Too flamboyant! Maggie smiles. Slowly but surely she is shedding her old, hesitant self. There's nothing wrong with flamboyant. On the contrary. You pay top dollar for a swimsuit, and it shows. The right people know what they're looking at when you walk past. They look at you as an equal, as one in the know.

She leans back in the chair. Ah, the water. Such a vast surface—all veneer. And ripples. Her thoughts roam free. She wants to go in, but is afraid of the water. Fear of water is a new thing with her. An image sneaks into her mind and she sees a scene from her childhood when she sat on the beach with her castle-building tools, and this large, disheveled woman walked right past her, a vacant expression on her broad, bland face. The way the woman looked, sort of wild and lost—an aberrant apparition on the quiet, suburban beach—little Maggie forgot all about her castle and watched the woman with great fascination. She saw her walk right into the water, having stopped only long enough to shed her clogs. The woman stepped into the water, and her dress, momentarily, swelled up like a balloon, then clung to her body for dear life. By then, little Maggie knew that something was wrong. She looked around her, thinking surely that someone would intervene, but nobody did. She called out to her mommy, "Look, look, she went into the water with her clothes on." And mommy, shading her eyes, raised her head from the newspaper and said, "That's all right, honey. Maybe she doesn't have a bathing suit."

It made sense, actually. And the woman did stop to shed her clogs—the sensible thing to do. But a little while later, everybody stood up on their feet, and the lifeguards rushed in and carried the woman out and laid her down on the sand and pumped water out of her lungs, and Maggie cried, and Maggie's mom cried, too.

Remembering her mother's face, Maggie cries now, lets the tears flow down her cheeks and onto her thighs. At first she worries that someone will notice, but nobody does, so she cries freely, glad for the tears; they purge away her fear, her anxiety.

She takes off her sunglasses and blows her nose, then

puts them back on.

Here, she is back to normal. The thought pleases her. Back to normal. As if she had gone somewhere and then came back.

Smiling, she looks out at the water and begins to laugh, she can't stop laughing. Hysterical, she buries her face in her bag and tells herself to calm down, calm down.

Here, she is calm, calm, no need to hide her face in the bag. She picks up her drink, sucks on the sweet, coconut drink and lights a cigarette. She takes a deep breath—whatever made her think of that poor woman? After all these years, how vividly she still lives in her memory. Memories. What a wondrous construction, maybe real, maybe not, or maybe a little of both. To think that so many images are stored away in her like so many treasures for her to pick and choose from at will. A world she can exist in, away from current demands and pressures.

The waiter appears, inquires politely if she is ready for another.

Yes, she is ready, she says, smiles up at him. Ever since she changed her hair, he looks at her differently, and the new swimsuit renders him speechless. Very much as he was when he gazed so helplessly at Robin. More importantly, now that she's been here a while, he treats her with respect, always comes over to see if she is all right, if she needs anything; she doesn't even have to wave him over. In a way, he encourages her to drink, just by asking if she is ready. And she, what can she say? Of course she is ready, she is always ready.

The waiter returns with a fresh drink, removes the old one. "Charge it to the room?"

"Please." How polite they all are. She's a woman of means, they treat her accordingly.

He lingers at her side. "Always the same book," he notes

with a smile.

She looks up at him, is glad she is wearing her sunglasses. She nods, she smiles, wills him to go away. But he doesn't. Stubbornly, it seems, he waits for her reply—why not indulge him?

She looks at the book. It's a library book, she remembers, now overdue, but they won't miss it. They have plenty of copies, or can order another. She remembers the dwarf, how he sang in the snow, his deep baritone voice transporting her to a place of longing. How long ago it seems.

"It's a souvenir," she says.

"A souvenir?"

"From a library."

"I see," he says, but she can see that he doesn't. She wants to start giggling again, but controls herself.

"Is it good?" he asks.

"Oh yes, very."

"You must like it."

Well, yes, she does, will he please go away and leave her alone? But she doesn't want to be rude, it's bad P.R. A little patience and forbearance never hurt anyone. "I do."

"How long are you going to stay with us?"

Through her glasses, she stares at him. Why is he asking her this? Is he spying on her on behalf of the manager? Mr. Darren called her the other day and asked the same exact question. He was courteous, of course, still she didn't appreciate his tone of voice. She could have said that as long as she pays her bills, he has no reason to complain, yet she didn't say it. But with this waiter here, she'd better be firm, if cordial, as befits a high-class guest.

"Why do you ask?"

He shrugs. "No reason."

"Well," she says. "I don't know, frankly."

"You're lucky," he says with no resentment in his voice. "You can take long vacations."

"Yes," she agrees.

At last he leaves, and she leans back in the chair. A couple of guys go by, one of them almost stumbles, looking at her. Now, with her new hair, she draws more glances from people, men and women alike—people notice her. It's almost as if she grew in stature, grew taller by a couple of inches. It must be true what they say, that blondes have more fun. How good it feels to have people look at you, perhaps envy you, your good looks, your wealth. And you can act as if you don't even see them, just walk past as if you were walking on air.

SHE VOMITS AT THE TABLE, WATCHES in frozen stupor as the dealer and the pit boss swiftly clean up the mess, expertly scrape off the vomit with paper towels, then rinse off the green felt with water. She is mortified. Will they punish her? Banish her from the casino?

Her eyes feel glassy, and she focuses hard on the pit boss and the dealer. She must appear sober, normal. But the two ignore her. More paper towels, more water. An ugly stain remains. Maggie thinks she detects an expression of loathing on the dealer's face: a haughty, angular blonde—a blue blood who must handle the vomit of drunk patrons.

How awful she feels! Thoroughly, unbearably ashamed. In fact, she's in shock, but it wasn't her fault, it wasn't. She can't understand how it happened, so sudden, and without warning. The stuff just came pouring out of her mouth, a torrent, had she tried, she could not have stopped.

How weird; she doesn't even remember getting drunk.

She is too embarrassed to look at the other players, to see their reaction and attempt to apologize. She has a sense that one or two of them leave the table in disgust, and the only thing for her to do is to ignore them, pretend she doesn't notice. These things happen, she tells herself. It can happen to anyone—no need to get so huffy, so indignant. The fact of the matter is, they're equipped in the casino for just such accidents. Here, the game resumes, the click-click-click of the shuffling machine.

What is she doing to her body? Is her brain still there?

Yes, it is. She can think rationally. It's been a very slow night, no real action, very few customers—must be a week-night. Thank God the two sisters she spoke to earlier are no longer there to witness her shame; they must have left, although she can't remember when. When she first joined the table, it was just the three of them, she and the two sisters. They hit it off right away. One of them, from Canada, came to visit her sister who lives in Nassau. "We haven't seen each other for twenty years," said the Canadian.

"Twenty years!" Maggie exclaimed. "That's a long time."

"That's right," said the Canadian, "but we're so much alike, we're getting to know each other, it's really amazing."

"Really? That's great," Maggie said, wondering if she sounded phony. The sisters were drinking white wine from tall glasses, and she remembers thinking how elegant the wine glasses looked; she, too, should have ordered white wine, rather than Bahama Mamas.

Should she leave the table? No, not yet. She can't leave now, shamefaced, defeated. If she leaves, they'll start discussing her and she won't be there to defend herself. Better act as if it didn't happen. Now that the poison is out of her system, she can see all right, and her head is clear. She needed to vomit, and she did. It must be something she ate. Indeed, if the front-desk people say something to her about this incident, she'll say it was probably food poisoning—they should be more careful with the food they serve. She can sue them, and it won't be a pleasant affair: their reputation is at stake.

Anyway, by now, at the table, the whole thing is forgotten, or should be. She doesn't care about these people, they don't know her, she'll never see them again. Already in their minds they've turned her into a curiosity they'll tell their friends about when they go back home. There's no room for weakness in the world. How quickly people pounce, how vehemently they assume a self-righteous attitude. She is all alone, she must stand her ground. When she is good and ready she'll leave this table and go to the bathroom to rest a little and freshen up. Then she'll find a friendly table where she'll engage a nice man in conversation. By now, she can spot them quite easily. It stands to reason: both she and they are easy targets.

SHE COUNTS HER MONEY. VERY CLOSE to three thousand. Twenty-eight hundred, to be exact. She is prosperous. She has yet to open a bank account, start saving for a rainy day. Not that it rains very much on the island.

She giggles. Counting her small fortune, she can't decide which she likes more: the smooth, shiny chips, or the crisp, one-hundred-dollar bills.

She has just woken up and is naked on the bed, Robin's bed. She is naked on the bed, arranging her assets in neat piles. Her hard-earned fortune, acquired with the sweat of her brow. Honest sweat. She vaguely remembers a story learned in childhood about an old miser always counting his capital, reveling in his wealth. There was a moral to the story, but she has forgotten it. Ah, well, it's not that important.

Her telephone rings—how unusual, her telephone never rings. She looks at the clock: ten in the morning. She won't answer it, pure and simple.

She gazes at the instrument. How persistent the ring is, it's driving her crazy. If she doesn't answer it, whoever is calling may come up to her door, which would be much worse. She picks up the receiver.

"Maggie! Maggie!"

What a pleasant surprise—Maggie wants to cackle. It is Robin's high voice, shrilling in her ear. "Maggie, do you hear me?"

"Huh, yes, Robin, of course I hear you, no need to shout." How calm she sounds compared to Robin, so calm and reserved.

Maggie smiles; she asks herself how soon she should hang up.

"What do you think you're doing?" The same shrill voice—how come she's never noticed this before? She is different from Robin, is more dignified, has better manners.

Maggie thinks a moment. She wonders where Robin is calling from.

"Where are you?" she asks, speaking slowly, softly.

"Where do you think? New York."

God, how common Robin sounds, how *ordinary*.

"Listen, Maggie, I have Susan on the line...."

Susan? Why did Robin have to involve Susan?

"Hi, Maggie, it's Susan," Susan says, sounding shy, guarded. "How are you?"

"I'm fine." Maggie feels a bit uncomfortable talking to Susan. "Are we having a conference call?" she inquires in a measured voice.

"When are you coming home?" Susan asks.

Home?

"Oh, Susan, I don't know, maybe soon. I met someone," she intimates.

"You met someone?" Susan repeats.

"Yes. He is very nice, very sweet to me."

"I don't believe her," Robin says.

"I thought you died, Robin," Maggie says to give Robin a little scare, and there's a long pause on the other end.

"Died?" Robin finally says. "What are you talking about?"

Maggie smiles; obviously, Robin finds the concept of her dying too distasteful. "Died," Maggie says. "Like, death, you know? They said something about the yacht. They said you drowned."

"That's totally absurd—"

"Anyway, what do you want, Robin? I can't talk very long, I have company."

"Company?!" Robin shrieks, and Maggie suppresses a giggle. "Listen, Mag, please listen to me. I feel terrible about what happened, and we can deal with it later. But right now

I want you to get on a plane and come home. If you like, I'll come and get you."

Maggie chuckles. "You're so funny, Robin. Thank you for calling. Susan, I'm sorry, I must go now. I'll call you sometime."

Gently, she puts down the receiver, tries to unplug the phone—impossible. She lies down on the bed and waits for it to ring again. It doesn't. Funny little Robin and her devious schemes, getting Susan on her side. Was Susan on Robin's side all along? No, of course not. She had told Robin about Susan, and Susan about Robin, but they never met. Robin probably called Maggie's office and asked to speak to Susan, so she wouldn't have to confront Maggie alone. It is all quite simple: poor little Robin must be green with envy. How come she never saw it? Never saw it was possible that Robin was envious of her?

Maggie checks her watch; incredibly, it's time for breakfast again. Is she hungry? Not really. A walk on the beach will do her good, some fresh air. Oh, yes, fresh air. How long has it been since she's had fresh air? Probably yesterday.

She laughs gaily. How silly of her to make such a fuss over a simple, available thing as fresh air. Quickly, she changes into her bathing suit and leaves the room. She drops her things on a chair and walks along the beach, her hands behind her back. How light she feels, almost weightless, almost like a child. It's so quiet, peaceful in her head, and the fine sand so warm under her feet. How good it feels to just walk along the beach with her hands behind her back. An onlooker may think she is deep in thought, and she is. Robin is desperate to insinuate herself back into Maggie's life, but Maggie won't allow it. Enough of the fake "sweetie" this and "sweetie" that. How she cringed every time Robin called her "sweetie." She cringed, and yet opened herself to believe that

Robin meant it, that there was a trust and a sisterly closeness between them.

She takes off her bathing suit and lies down on the sand, digging herself deeper into the enveloping warmth. There are bushes above her in the dunes, and not a soul in sight. She wants to hug herself, hug mounds of sand to her chest. Sand, more sand, she can't have enough. And now a small cushion to lay down her head and doze off for a while. A large sand crab, only a few inches away, half emerges from its hole. Its black, shiny eyes, stationed on two stubby antennae, register her presence, or so she thinks. She wills it to come out and go about its business, but it quickly retreats. She remains still, watching the hole. Her patience pays off. The crab reappears, venturing further up at the mouth of the hole, a lump of wet sand neatly packed under one of its legs. It tosses out the sand and goes back inside. The crab, she muses, is remodeling its home. Indeed, here it comes again, hurling more sand and hurrying indoors, only to reappear with a new load. She marvels at its single-minded efficiency, packing quite a bit of sand under its tiny leg. It would take so little to destroy its home, bury the crab alive—she wonders if it's all alone down below. Is it a female, perhaps, preparing to lay her eggs?

Maggie digs deeper into her pile of sand. She has tired of watching the crab, the loner. She rests her head. If only she could turn over and go to sleep, right here, next to the crab's hole. Under the bright sun, her blond hair, like a doll's, blends beautifully with the sand. Her skin, too, where exposed, has taken the golden hue of sand; she bakes in a sand oven. Would someone, please, poke a finger to check if she's good enough to eat? This thought brings a smile to her lips. She'll rest here a while then go back to her room, her sanctuary.

SHE PUTS ON MAKEUP, TURNS HER FACE into an impervious mask. It's seven o'clock in the evening, and she feels a little harried; she has work to do. A pack of freeloaders hangs about her, waiting for payoffs. They're dependent on her, and she is generous. One might say she's the responsible head of a large industry, keeping everybody afloat.

She sits down at the bar and orders a drink. It's another way of doing business. If nothing happens, she may tour the tables, play roulette, or Caribbean Poker. For now, it feels nice to just sit and relax. The long round bar overlooks the casino, and she can watch the crowds as they come in.

It's still early. At this hour, people eat dinner, prepare for the night. She is alone at the bar, and Carlos, the bartender, keeps her company. His mother, he tells her, is in the hospital, and she nods, wondering if she should give him a couple of quarter chips to buy something for his mother. That's what she'll do. When she tips him, she'll set aside the green chips, say, This is for your mother; Carlos won't refuse her.

Very few tables are open, and most of the activity is at the slots. The casino is nice and quiet, almost empty—like a shrine before prayer time. Must be Monday, she reflects. Most of the weekend's guests have left, and new fresh blood will soon arrive, hopefully tomorrow.

"Is it Monday?" she asks Carlos, and he confirms with a smile. She wonders if Carlos wonders about her. He never asks her any questions, has no demands of her. She is touched by the fact that he is gentle with her, so respectful, and so polite—it nearly moves her to tears. Tears, naturally, are absurd. She hasn't cried in a while, had no reason to.

As she watches, a group of young girls bursts into the casino, and Maggie observes them. Slim, and variously blond, they're wearing T-shirts and shorts, laughing their free, American laugh. They're a vague reminder of a life she once had, which makes her feel yet more estranged from them. High school graduates, she surmises, whose well-to-do parents paid for a fun trip. Those parents, Maggie reflects, had better be more vigilant; there's no safety in numbers.

One of the girls shrieks, "I'll take the Fifth," and her friends crack up. Maggie glances at Carlos. He smiles, shrugs, he's seen it all before. He takes her empty glass, puts a fresh drink before her: whiskey-sour. All at once, she feels old, unattractive.

"I'll be right back," she murmurs, makes her way to the bathroom. She leans close to the mirror. In the mirror she looks fine, even great. Just as ripe and seasoned as the Brazilian with the freckles in the short black dress—what is the matter with her?

Appeased, she goes back to the bar. A man is seated one chair over from hers. A navy-blue jacket over a white shirt. Casual, but elegant. In his fifties or sixties. An expensive gold watch, a silver cigarette case. Perfect. Possibly, an all-nighter. Dinner included, some gambling at a table of his choice.

She sits down, acknowledges him with her special smile—generous, wide-mouthed—a smile she has practiced long and hard before the mirror. Carlos, discreetly, removes himself to the other end of the bar.

"It's so quiet tonight." She speaks softly, holds a cigarette up for him to light. Naturally, the man reaches for his lighter. She leans toward the flame, throws her head back, exhaling.

"You are very beautiful," says the man. A heavy accent. Dutch? German? An image flashes in her mind: she is in the hospital, feeding strawberries to her mother, hoping to cure her of the cancer. Days and nights she sat there, at her mother's bed, accompanying her to her death.

"My mother," she says, and the man regards her, a strange look in his eyes.

"Your mother?"

"My mother," she says, dreamily, "was very beautiful. She is dead now."

"Oh, I am sorry." He seems to lose interest; he seems to think there was some mistake.

"It's all right, it happened so long ago." Maggie smiles. "She used to touch me, like this, very gently." Maggie stretches out her arm across the bar and, with her other hand, begins to caress her skin, looking all the while into the man's eyes. "Like this....very softly...." She smiles. "Look, there's still some sand on my skin, very fine sand. This morning, I took off my bathing suit and lay on the beach all by myself. It felt so nice, so warm."

The man just looks at her, he doesn't get it. What's wrong with him?

"I feel alone tonight," she says. "Will you have dinner with me?"

The man glances at his watch. "I am sorry, but it is impossible."

"How about a drink up in my room? I have a beautiful room, with two double beds. You can see the ocean."

"A drink?" He frowns, not understanding. Then he understands; he shifts in his chair. "How much?"

Too blunt for her taste, but she'll take him anyway. She proffers a smile. "I'm sure we'll agree."

"No, no." He is adamant. "You must tell me now."

A real prick, she thinks. "Five hundred?"

The German is shocked, his pale eyes bulge in their sockets. "You are crazy," he exclaims with his stupid accent, and she is furious.

"Fuck you," she shouts and stands up. She must control

herself, mustn't create a scene, but she is trembling with rage. "You fucking Nazi."

Carlos, alarmed, begins to approach them, and the man points at her, mumbling, "She....she...."

"She, she," she mimics and begins to laugh. "This guy is a nut," she tells Carlos as she walks away. "Better watch out."

The guy stands up and wiggles his finger. "Whore, whore," he blurts in his absurd, moronic accent. A few heads turn, but she continues on. She worries that perhaps the guy is following her, but she doesn't dare to turn around to check. She must appear oblivious; there's nothing between her and that crazy man. Ah, she would have loved to put him in his place, but the guy is a lunatic, he could be dangerous; she'd better not get mixed up with him.

Up in the room she is trembling, pacing. The guy's a psychopath, clearly. And the gall, calling her a whore. What a strange concept, a whore. And what's wrong with a whore anyway? It's the oldest profession. Besides, if there were no men in the world, there would be no whores. She'd better stop pacing, or she'll go mad.

She stands, staring at herself in the mirror, furiously puffing on her cigarette. Perceiving herself in such a sorry state, she wants to break down and cry. Her eyes are ready to fill up with tears, but she feels a hardness inside which won't allow her to break down. A whore, he said, a whore. How about the little wife? she could have yelled in response, but it's a good thing she didn't, the guy is obviously deranged, a lunatic. How could she have mistaken a lunatic for a man who would be good to her, who would treat her nicely? Is she losing it? No, she's not losing anything. Here, she's made herself a drink, she is sitting down in front of the mirror. Here, she is calm, she has calmed down, she is combing her hair, her big brown eyes meeting her gaze in the mirror. She made a mistake, it won't happen again, all she needs to do is erase the whole episode from her mind.

But what if Carlos tells Mr. Darren, the manager, about this little incident? In her confusion, she never got to tip him like she meant to. She'll go downstairs later and talk to him. Carlos is on her side. He is not the type to meddle in other people's affairs. Bartenders get to witness all sorts of weird scenes, it's part of the trade; they're trained to watch and keep the peace.

But what if the guy goes and complains? No, he won't. What can he complain about? All she did was offer him a drink. He's the one who should be worried, calling her a whore: she can sue him for slander. That's right, slander. And her hair is all wrong, and so is her face. In fact, her face is boring, it's time she changed it.

BREAKFAST IN BED. A LIFE-LONG fantasy come true. How wonderful it is to be able to indulge when you feel like it. She used to take her breakfast downstairs, in the restaurant, but not anymore. It's so much nicer up here, in her room, where she doesn't have to deal with people she doesn't wish to see. Like Mr. Darren, the all-important hotel manager who has been pestering her. He says they need her room, a big convention will be arriving soon, as if it's any of her concern. He's a nice enough man, this Mr. Darren, a native, but not very bright. He gives her strange looks which she can't decipher. Maybe he's attracted to her but doesn't know how to express it, he being so black and she so white and blond. Yesterday, with a silent Wynston at his side, he tried a new tactic, asking her all sorts of questions. Such a nosey busybody. If he doesn't stop, she'll have to complain to his supervisors. Even managers have supervisors, she'll go right to the top. This is a large hotel, eleven hundred rooms. Let Mr. Darren bother his head about the other guests.

Now she waits for the room-service waiter to bring in her tray. Soon he arrives, places the tray on the table. She signs the check, then hands him a quarter chip, which he takes without a word and puts in his pocket. You'd think it's coming to him. The first couple of times, though, he was quite impressed, quite appreciative. Starting tomorrow, she'll have to give him a little more to keep him happy. Money no longer means much—she has plenty. And she is generous, doesn't mind sharing her good fortune.

She takes her breakfast to Robin's bed and turns on the TV. For background noise. She doesn't pay attention to what they're saying, but she likes to gaze at the moving pictures, especially at the faces. The voices of people are like music to her ears—people talking, debating, arguing, as if something important is taking place.

She'll stay in bed today, relax, take it easy. She can afford to take a day off. Even two days off.

She looks at the tray. A small pot of coffee, fruit salad, cottage cheese, a pitcher of cold water. She is very good when it comes to her diet. And she is never really hungry anymore: she puts food in her mouth because one has to. Slowly, she spoons the fruit salad, the cheese, chews. Already she looks forward to what she'll do after breakfast: make herself a light drink and smoke a cigarette.

She puts away the tray and prepares a drink of vodka and juice. Lots of ice. Drink in hand, she sashays around the room, willing a booklet of matches to materialize—on the table, the commode, in one of the ashtrays. It's a cursory search, indolent, for she is certain that such a small detail, a match, won't stand between her and total contentment.

She can't find any. Instantly, she panics. Frantic, she goes through her purse, the drawers, finally finds a booklet in the bathroom. What a relief!

She lights a cigarette, inhales deeply, sips her drink. She looks in the mirror, smiles. She has to laugh at herself. How quickly she loses it when it seems, even briefly, that she won't be able to secure her pleasure. How elementary she has become, so militant, so focused on her needs. One would think she were destitute, but of course she isn't. She has close to four grand in the drawer. While Robin, fat, little Robin, is slaving away at her lousy job with CBS, or is sucking good old balding Ben.

She looks in the mirror, lights another cigarette. She likes to sit and smoke, watch herself in the mirror; it soothes and relaxes her. She likes to watch herself think, she likes to watch herself admiring herself. Like she does now. She has dyed her hair again—just the right shade of blond and not as metallic as before. Sip, inhale. A quiet moment. She will never tire of looking at the reflection of her own face. By now, she's gotten used to her new look and can't even remember what she looked like before. It would be a pity, hiding such a beauty up in her room. Maybe she will go down, after all. Later tonight.

FLOWERS, YES! FRESH FLOWERS. A comfort to the eyes. Leafing through a magazine, she comes upon a picture of Brooke Astor with her schnauzer, Maizie, and her dachshund, Dolly. In the photograph, even the dogs seem to know they're aristocrats. In the background, a beautiful bouquet of flowers sprouting from the mouth of a gorgeous vase. Such beautiful, bright colors. How come she hasn't thought about this before? It's as if she had forgotten there were flowers in the world.

She picks up the phone, calls the front desk, asks them to deliver fresh flowers to her room.

She hears whispering on the line: what are they whispering about?

"What kind of flowers?" the clerk finally asks.

"Beautiful flowers," she says. "Send up a nice bouquet. Two bouquets, in fact. One for the commode, and one for the table."

She looks at her watch. Seven-thirty. Time to go down. She's learned a new game, baccarat, where cards are dealt to her, and she doesn't have to think much. High rollers play baccarat, it's a classy game. She meets classy people, men who honor their word and treat her with respect. The kind of men who appreciate flowers in a home. Men who allow her to cuddle up, pretend she's in love. She has bought a few more dresses in one of the shops in the hotel, and has now a whole new wardrobe. Tonight she is wearing a silky black dress, so soft and well cut, it fits her superbly. And in her black, satin shoes with the very high heels, and in her new hair, cascading down to her shoulders, and her new gold earrings and necklace, she is a sight to behold, a real knockout. Stunning, absolutely stunning. She has learned to affect a certain pose, like a mannequin in a window, allowing a slight curve to her body with her pelvis thrust forward. Like she stands now, in front of the mirror, moving her hands down her waist, her thighs. So slim, so slender, so with it. She has lost some weight, but can afford to lose more. She has developed a new relationship with her body and now observes it with expert detachment. Very much like a model would, or an athlete. One way or the other, they are all in the market, competing for excellence and distinction in their fields.

THERE'S A LOUD KNOCK ON HER DOOR. Maggie comes out of the bathroom and opens it. A maid is in the hall with her cart. She wants to make up the room, she says.

"Come back later," Maggie mutters and shuts the door. She is not ready, not yet.

"But, Miss," she hears the maid's muffled voice from the other side. "It's already three o'clock."

"Come back tomorrow," Maggie says and looks around her. What a mess. The breakfast tray is on the floor, a couple of wet towels. Her chips from last night and several crumpled bills are scattered on the bedspread on Robin's bed. Robin's bed—she smiles. It is her bed now. One bed to sleep in, one bed to count her money on. Some time ago, they tried to move her to another room with only one bed, but she said, No, this is my room. This room brings me luck, I must stay here.

She goes to her bed and lies down. She feels lethargic,

perhaps exhausted. Did she have breakfast, and then doze off? The more she sleeps, the more tired she is. She hasn't gone out to the beach, as she normally does, but she might later. It's only three o'clock. Or, she might just stay in the room, take the day, the night, off.

She shuts her eyes. Agreeable thoughts roam in her head. She can't say what they are. She can only say that their texture is pleasant.

Again, a knock on the door. What do they want from her? Why won't they leave her alone? Can't they read English? The 'Do Not Disturb' sign is hanging outside from the doorjamb.

"Who is it?" she calls.

"It's me, Sophia." Sophia, her favorite maid. "May I come in, Miss?"

"All right, come in."

She hears the key in the lock, and Sophia appears. She goes to the glass doors and opens them wide. A warm breeze comes in from the veranda. "It smells in here, Miss," she tells Maggie in a low voice.

Maggie isn't hurt. Sophia hasn't accused her of anything. In fact, Sophia seems mortified for having said such a thing.

"I don't smell anything." Maggie smiles, looks over at the other bed where last night's harvest is in full view. Probably more than Sophia's monthly wages. She notices a used condom on the floor; Sophia, she knows, has noticed it, too.

"Let me clean the room, Miss. You'll feel much better."

"What's the problem, Sophia? So it won't be cleaned."

"It's been two days, Miss."

"Two days? Are you sure?"

"I'm sure, Miss. Two days."

"Two days," Maggie considers. "I wonder. Help me, Sophia."

Sophia helps her out of bed. "No good to keep your money like that." Sophia points at the chips.

"I wonder," Maggie says. "Did I have breakfast this morning?"

"I don't know, Miss. Maybe yesterday."

"Maybe yesterday. The brain, the brain." She points at her head, and Sophia laughs. It's good, she thinks, that she can make someone laugh. "Nice name, Sophia, I like Sophia." She picks a couple of quarter chips off the bed and hands them to the maid.

"No, no, no," Sophia says, obviously confounded by the large tip.

"Yes, yes, yes," Maggie says, reaching for Sophia's hand.

But Sophia recoils, pulls her hand back. "Manager no like...."

Maggie shakes her head. Softly, she says, "Don't worry about the manager, Sophia. Here." She takes Sophia's hand and puts the chips in her palm. "This is for you. Go buy yourself something."

"Thank you, Miss."

She is being nice to them all—why? Because she is nice, she is a nice person, and generous, too. And it makes her feel good. There's plenty of cash to go around—why not share it, keep everybody happy?

The maid is still standing there, the chips in her hand. She seems to have something on her mind.

"What is it, Sophia? Why are you looking at me like this?"

"Not happy, the manager." She points at the money on the bed.

Maggie laughs. "Of course he's not happy. It's casino money. I'm too lucky for him."

"No, no," Sophia says.

"Yes, yes, Sophia, not to worry. Brain still here." She points at her forehead, but Sophia won't laugh.

"Manager say you go away."

"Good. Let him go away, he may need a rest."

"No, no—"

"Yes, yes, Sophia, I told you *not to worry*. Who does he think he is, anyway?" She raises her voice a little. "He's a low-level clerk, that's what he is. Now, let's see. I need fresh flowers for my room. As you can see, these are dead." She plucks a couple of tissues from the box, and picks up the condom. "Now, don't just stand there, Sophia," she reprimands softly. "You wanted to clean the room, so go ahead, clean it."

"Yes, Miss."

S HE STANDS NEAR THE WATER, WATCHING the couple she's been spying on all morning. Earlier, they were sitting a few feet away from her, and she watched them, sprawled on their chairs, smoking, sipping coke, fishing potato chips from a bag. The woman, an attractive redhead in a tight, silver bikini, was wearing her earrings and bracelets, which gave Maggie the idea she might do the same in the future, starting tomorrow. She doesn't go into the water anymore, so she might as well look her best, donning her jewelry. The guy, sort of chubby and clumsy-looking, didn't seem, physically at least, to be the right partner for the redhead, and

Maggie wondered why the woman married him. Money? Yet, there seemed to be a nice rapport between them, the way they lit each other's cigarettes, passed the coke and the bag of potato chips between them. Perhaps it is true love, Maggie thought.

Then they got up and went into the water, and she followed behind and now stands, at the edge of the water, and watches them. They don't seem to have noticed her. They lie, face down, on two inflated rafts the hotel provides. She could take one, too, and float, like them, on the water, but such a simple form of diversion doesn't appeal to her. She asks herself if they do this out of boredom, but then concludes that people in love are like children: as long as they're together, they'll find pleasure in nearly everything they do. She tries to remember if she and Tom acted this way, but it's light-years away....

"Hello, Maggie," someone says, handing her a drink. "It's your favorite," he says. "Bahama Mama."

"Bahama Mama." She smiles, takes the drink from his hand. A nice-looking man, thirtyish, in bathing trunks, swarthy, a little paunchy in the middle, but she has seen worse. A pinky diamond ring.

"A beautiful day," he says, and she looks up to the sky and says, Yes, it is. He leads her back to her chair under the umbrella, lights a cigarette for her. So attentive, so outgoing, so sure of himself. If she set her mind to it, she could think of him as her type, she could even love him. She shows him the book she is reading.

"A good book?" he asks.

"Very," she says. He seems only mildly interested, but he is courting her. It's been so long since someone courted her. Obviously, books are not essential in his life, but with time he'll change, if only to please her.

She sips the drink he has bought for her. So cool, so refreshing, and soothing. "Have you read him?" she asks, and again he looks at the cover, shakes his head, No.

"He is very avant garde," she says.

"Really?" He moves his hand up and down her arm. He seems distracted. If he stroked her with more intent, he could have aroused her.

Coquettishly, she asks, "How come you know my name?"

He looks at her, is somewhat puzzled. "How about if we go upstairs for a little while," he says.

"Upstairs? Where?"

"Your room, Maggie, I don't have much time." He points at his watch, one of those bulky ones.

"Oh," she says, blushes terribly, hopes he doesn't notice. Now she understands. He must be someone she's been with, maybe last night, maybe the night before. She is not drunk yet, but she can do this sober if she has to.

She gulps down the drink, gathers up her things, and the man tells her he'll meet her in the room, he needs to get his wallet. Upstairs, she takes off her bathing suit and lies on the bed. He arrives with his wallet and tosses it on the table, quickly peels off his trunks. He is more than just a little paunchy, and is quite hairy—how could she possibly imagine, even for a second, that he might be her type? That she could love him? The good thing: he's already erect. If only he knew how ridiculous he looks with his little pecker sticking out from below the hairy belly. This one, she knows, won't last very long.

She leans over, gets a condom from the drawer. He penetrates her and, for a split second, she is reminded of the other kind of sex she used to fantasize about, where her body would fill up with need, with desire, with pleasure, as she held a man close to her.

He moves on top of her, grunts, and is finished. After he leaves, she decides, she'll masturbate.

He pulls out of her and gets off the bed, picking up his things. His big, hairy ass, his fat thighs are so revolting, she wants to puke. And his dangling, wet pecker, with the condom still drooping from it. As soon as he leaves, she'll call Housekeeping, have them change the sheets. In the meantime, she stays right where she is, leaning on her elbow, watching him. He pulls off the condom and drops it to the floor, then, standing on one foot, he thrusts his leg through the trunks. He loses his balance, hops a moment, then finally succeeds.

Maggie leans back, covers her face, laughing.

"I wouldn't laugh if I were you," she hears him say.

"No?" She hugs her knees, feeling like a twelve-year-old. "Why not?"

"Because." He opens his wallet and tosses a few bills on the bed. "They're on to you, sweetheart. Better get off your high horse and pack your things. If you want my advice."

"I don't want your advice," she says, but anxiety begins to creep up her chest.

"You do as you please, sweetie-pie. I'm doing you a favor telling you this." He begins to walk to the door.

"Wait a minute." She jumps out of bed. "He sent you, didn't he?" She smiles at him mischievously.

"Who?"

"You know who. Mr. Darren."

The man laughs. "Nobody sent me."

"Tell him that if he gives me a hard time, I'll move to another hotel. They'll lose my business, and I'll sue them for harassment."

"My advice to you, Maggie." He turns, smiling crookedly at her. The way he says her name, so precisely, and yet friendly, makes her want to listen to him. "Go away, quietly, don't make any scenes. They can lock you up, you know?"

"Lock me up?" This is an entirely new thought.

"Absolutely. Think about it." He opens the door, blows her a kiss and then is gone.

Outside the glass doors, the sun shines brightly, almost too brightly. In this light, the peachy walls and bedspreads nauseate her. She draws the curtains. Lock her up? Preposterous, the guy is crazy. But what if he is telling her the truth?

If he is telling the truth, she'd better prepare for them.

Prepare for them? How?

She is driving herself nuts, and for no reason. Indeed, they're somewhat primitive on this island, but lock her up? On what charges? She is not a criminal. It's quite clear: she laughed at the guy, and he was just looking to hurt her. Or, Darren had sent him to scare her off, but she doesn't scare that easily. Darren is her enemy, he's on her case. Sooner or later, she'd have to deal with him.

She picks up the bills from the bed and puts them in the drawer. The truth is, she's been too anxious lately, too restless. Something has been eating at her—but what? For now, she'd better rest, take a little nap and clear her head. She could take the day off, and maybe she will. If Sophia appears with her clanky cart, she'll send her away.

SHE COUNTS HER MONEY. SHE HAS LESS than $2,000 in her cache, which is very disquieting. Do the maids go into her drawers and steal from her? No. Her capital is dwindling because she overspends and overtips. Maybe she shouldn't tip so lavishly—it only makes her suspect in their eyes—but it's too late to stop now. Somehow, she must start economizing. It's not an immediate worry, her bills are paid up, but it's something she'd better start thinking about.

But she doesn't want to think about it. She has made plans for the day and intends to carry them out. Today, Sunday, she'll go out on a tour. She needs to get away, she is tired of the casino, she deserves a rest. She'll pack her bathing suit, go somewhere where nobody knows her. She'll get off Paradise Island, go visit New Providence, tour Nassau. She'll be dressed all in white—a white sparkling flower in this green, tropical landscape. She'll wear the white cotton pants and shirt she bought especially for the trip before leaving New York. She is the lady in white, will always be thought of as the lady in white.

She comes out of the hotel, blinks against the bright sun. She looks for her sunglasses in her bag. She must have left them upstairs, but has no time to lose. She waves, No, at the cab drivers who offer their services and sets out on foot.

How green and lush everything is. No wonder celebrities spend millions, building their villas here. Natives don't live on Paradise Island, only wealthy foreigners. Of course, you never see them. They build their villas and let the Mercedeses and Porsches sit shiny and useless in the spacious garages for most of the year.

How light she feels! Her clothes hang on her body, loose, inconsequential. Has she lost more weight? Possibly. She likes to think she's a skeleton, her shirt, her pants, mere coverings.

She arrives at the bridge to New Providence. It's a long walk across, but she doesn't mind it. On the contrary, she seeks the physical exertion.

How beautiful the sky is, and the water all around. A couple of native women cross the bridge with her. Too bad she hasn't thought of taking a hat; the sun, right on top of her, is a white, fiery hoop.

Here she is, on the other side. She boards a bus full of natives and sits up front, right behind a young boy. "How much is the fare?" she asks the boy in a whisper. He turns to her, and in a grave, adult manner tells her it's a dollar, but that she doesn't have to pay now, only when she gets off. Charmed by his solemnity, she murmurs, "Thank you," and relaxes back in the seat.

The bus, in fact, is a mini van. There are designated bus stops, but it seems that the driver stops anywhere people want to get off, or whenever they flag him on the road. Indeed, passengers pay as they get off: bills the driver stuffs in his pocket, coins he drops in a slot. Such a casual arrangement amazes her: how does the bus company keep him honest? Perhaps, she decides, each bus operator is on his own—much like a cabbie in New York.

How good she feels on the bus, with the breeze blowing her hair, caressing her face. The neighborhoods they drive through appear to be dirt-poor, with shacks and huts strewn about randomly, yet people sit under trees in their front yards and talk and laugh: it's lunch time on Sunday and people visit, their kids running about, chasing each other.

Her stomach growls—if only she could get off and join them. How much simpler their lives are. Clean, wholesome. She could easily adapt to such a life, it is not too late.

She studies the natives on the bus: they don't question

her presence among them. Those who work at the hotel are different—they are more aggressive, aloof, even hostile, perhaps because they have to deal with whites every day of the year, whites who demand service as if the world belonged to them, this island included.

She studies her fellow-passengers and marvels at their relaxed demeanor; no one seems hassled or harried. They seem respectful of each other, accepting, non-judgmental. A young mother, seated across from her, kisses her baby daughter smack on the mouth—a quick peck of pure emotion expressed simply, instinctively. Maggie devours them with her eyes, she can't have enough.

O N THE SAND, ON SOME PUBLIC beach in Nassau, Maggie sits. There are no umbrellas, and the sun is beating down on her. Again she regrets not having brought a hat. There's a fisherman in the water, trying to catch a fish. A bit farther in the distance, a buoy calmly bobs with the wind. There are a few people scattered here and there on blankets on the sand, all of them natives, picnicking. She probably stands out, the only white among them.

Unlike the enclosed, artificial strip of sand at the hotel, this beach is pristine, with bushes sprouting up in the dunes. It feels more like a real beach, with a couple of kids in the water, splashing and screaming, with mothers and fathers getting sandwiches and fruit out of plastic bags. She could go up to one of the families, perhaps be invited to share their food. Has she eaten today? She can't remember. The horizon is so still, it shimmers. She is tempted to go into the water and cool off, but is still afraid, or is she?

She stands up and walks to the water. How pure it looks, and so inviting. Why did she stay away for so long? What was she afraid of? Here, she has reached it, her feet are submerged, so nice and tan and glistening under the clear, sparkling water. A funny sensation on her skin, near her ankles, sort of ticklish, coolish, but not unpleasant; it's only water, she has always liked the water.

She wiggles her toes, contemplates the shiny red polish. Yes, the polish is shiny, but its shine looks caked, foreign on her nails. She must remember to remove it as soon as she gets home.

She takes another step, then another. She feels buoyant in the water, almost weightless. She forgot how soothing the water is! She is the innocent newborn, starting her life afresh. She will swim out to where it's so unbelievably peaceful, so calm, and the water is real clear and cleansing. She will float a while, then swim back to shore, sit down with one of the families and share their simple, wholesome lunch.

Swiftly, the water closes in on her—she can feel her heart pound in her chest. The fabric of her clothes, now transparent, adheres to her body like a new skin. A new sense of joy overtakes her and she wants to laugh, but her voice, still uncertain, catches in her throat. She is somewhat embarrassed by the nagging thought that the natives on the beach are perhaps watching, perhaps wondering what she is up to, wading in the water, fully clothed. But, it's quite simple: she forgot to bring her swimsuit! Which, when you think of it, is all for the better. Her swimsuit is all wrong, too daring, too showy, inappropriate for this tranquil beach, or for swimming.

She looks out to the buoy. Yes, she'll swim there and wait a while. Someone from shore is bound to notice her all alone in the deep. Someone from shore is bound to come out and rescue her. She needs to be rescued, she wants to be.

TSIPI KELLER was born in Prague, raised in Israel, and
has been living in New York since 1974. Her short fiction,
and her poetry translations, have appeared in many
journals and anthologies; her novels, *The Prophet of Tenth
Street* (1995) and *Leverage* (1997) were translated into
Hebrew and published by Sifriat Poalim. Keller's translation of Dan Pagis's posthumous collection, Last Poems,
was published by The Quarterly Review of Literature
(1993), and her translation of Irit Katzir's posthumous
collection, *And I Wrote Poems*, was published by Carmel in
2000. Among her awards are A National Endowment for
the Arts fellowship, a New York Foundation for the Arts
grant, and an Armand G. Erpf award from Columbia
University.

S P U Y T E N   D U Y V I L

All Spuyten Duyvil titles are in print and
available through your local bookseller via Booksense.com

Distributed to the trade by
Biblio Distribution
a division of NBN
1-800-462-6420
http://bibliodistribution.com

All Spuyten Duyvil authors may be contacted at
authors@spuytenduyvil.net

Author appearance information and background at
http://spuytenduyvil.net

Keller, Tsipi.
Jackpot :